THE YULETIDE HAUNTING AT LIVINGSTON MANOR

CAT KNIGHT

Disclaimer

This story is a work of fiction, any resemblance to people is purely coincidence. All places, names, events, businesses, etc. are used in a fictional manner. All characters are from the imagination of the author.

Table of Contents

Prologue

As Lord Livingston pulled away from the lights of London, he silently prayed he would make it to the manor house safely. A wicked wind whipped the thick snow across the road, making it almost impossible to see. Already, the road was snow-covered and dangerous. He slowed automatically and turned up the heater. It seemed as if the cold had seeped right through the windows, and it was terribly cold.

His late father would have pronounced the night unfit for "man or beast". It was the sort of night where everything that wanted to live would find some sort of shelter. The creatures that failed to keep warm would be found the next day, frozen and dead. He slowed still more as the road disappeared in front of him. He didn't have far to go, but a mile in a blizzard was a terribly long distance to walk.

The week before Christmas was unusually cold and snowy, but the weather rarely cooperated with the holiday cheer. Lord Livingston was happy to be going home, away from the lights and bustle of London. Time spent in the country would rejuvenate him, he might even host a New Year's Eve party.

He was creeping along when he spotted the man.

Man?

At first, Lord Livingston couldn't believe his eyes. Surely, the whirling snow was playing havoc with his sight. But he stopped anyway and waited. Seconds later, the door opened, and a man, a shivering man, loaded himself into the car.

"What the bloody hell are you doing out on a night like this?" Lord Livingston asked.

"Thank ye for stopping," the man said. "I'm trying to reach Liverpool."

"In weather like this? Are you daft?"

In the warm car, the man gave off a decidedly foul odour, as if he hadn't bathed in a century. Lord Livingston wanted to crack his window, but he thought that would be an obvious snub.

"I don't keep up with the news," the man answered. "And it wasn't so bad when I left London."

"And someone dropped you off out here?"

"It was as far as he was going."

Lord Livingston knew why the man was out in the snow and cold. He was a vagrant, someone who didn't work, who lived on the dole. The smell and the ragged clothes gave away the game.

"What's in Liverpool?" Lord Livingston asked.

"A friend. He has a place where I can hole up for a week or two."

"A job?"

"Maybe."

Lord Livingston knew the man was lying, but it wasn't a terrible lie. The man might have some sort of menial job waiting. Lord Livingston was prone to generosity so close to Christmas. No one wanted to be a Scrooge.

"No matter," Lord Livingston said. "You can spend the night in the manor house and be on your way in the morning."

"That is right nice of you," the man said. "And I thank ye. I was beginning to lose feeling in me toes."

Lord Livingston declined to comment on the status of the man's toes or fingers or nose or whatever else had been open to the elements.

"What is your name?" Lord Livingston asked.

"Parker, Stan Parker."

"Well, Mr. Parker, sit back and relax. The manor isn't far away, but in this filthy weather, it will take some minutes to get there."

"I'm in no hurry. Take your time."

Lord Livingston heard a note of condescension in the man's voice, and it bothered the lord. Why was a vagrant granting leave to a lord? It was wrong, but Lord Livingston was not going to ruin his Christmas mood. After all, he had done the charitable thing. Parker was going to spend the night in the manor, probably the best home Parker had ever known.

Lord Livingston didn't bother trying to put the car in the garage. He pulled to the front and stopped.

"Come along, Parker, while we can still see the house."

Together, they waded through the snow and into the house. In the entry, they shook the snow off their shoulders.

Lord Livingston expected one of the help to come for their coats, but no one did. He took his and the rag that smelled like a stockyard and hung them on the coat rack to dry. He told himself that he would have to have his coat cleaned after this night, probably the car too. There was no telling what sort of vermin Parker had brought with him. With any luck, Parker's infestation would be confined to a few, select rooms.

"Well, hello, we have company."

Lord Livingston turned to his wife who kissed his cheek.

"Yes," Lord Livingston said. "This is Mr. Parker. I found him on the road, and this is no night to be out. I promised him he could stay the night. Mr. Parker, this is Lady Livingston."

"Pleased to meet ya," Parker said. "And I thank ya for the bed. I was a bit desperate out there."

Lord Livingston noticed that Parker carried a small bag, probably holding everything the beggar owned. Lord Livingston told himself that in the morning, he would augment the poor man's wardrobe. At least then he would smell better.

"Dinner is almost ready," Lady Livingston said. "And there is plenty. Would you like to freshen up, Mr. Parker?" The man grinned, and Lord Livingston noted the growth of beard.

The man's best teeth were yellow and the rest... Lord Livingston guessed that the man hadn't seen a dentist in a decade at least.

"That would suit me fine," Parker said.

"Follow me," Lady Livingston said.

Lord Livingston watched the two disappear upstairs before he marched into the library and poured himself a stiff whiskey. He downed it quickly and savoured the heat. By God, he was going to get warm one way or another. He was halfway through his second glass when Lady Livingston returned.

"You do find them, don't you," she said as he poured her a drink.

"What was I to do? It's a deadly night out there, and this is Christmas week, isn't it?"

"A bath will do the man a lot of good, but I'm afraid the smell is in the clothes also."

"We can bear up for one night. He'll be gone in the morning."

"Along with the silver."

They both laughed as their small terrier ran into the room.

"Where have you been?" Lord Livingston asked as he bent over to rub the dog's ears.

"Don't pet him," Lady Livingston said. "When I put him out earlier, he did not wish to come back in. I had to put on my boots and retrieve him."

"Too much attention," Lord Livingston said. "Shut the door and in five minutes, he'll be scratching to be let in. Dogs are not fools. Where is everyone?"

"I let the help go early because of the storm," Lady Livingston said. "It's just us."

"And Mr. Parker."

"Yes, well, him."

Lord Livingston was on his third whiskey when Parker entered the room. True to Lady Livingston's prediction, Parker did not smell appreciatively better despite the bath. But he did accept the whiskey which he polished off in one quick drink. Lord Livingston had no choice but the refresh the glass. Before Parker could slam down the second glass, Lady Livingston shepherded them into the dining room.

They had no sooner entered the room when the dog raced in, barking, and growling at Parker. While the little dog hopped around in a tizzy, biting at Parker's pants, the man tried to kick it.

"Here now," Lord Livingston said. "That's uncalled for."

"The little nipper's trying to bite me."

"He's hardly a threat," Lady Livingston said as she gathered up the dog.

"If you had been chased as much as me," Parker answered. "You'd kick the rascal clear across the room."

"He's gone," Lord Livingston said. "Why don't you sit down."

"If he gets loose, I'll protect myself," Parker said as he sat.

"He won't get loose."

In a minute, Lady Parker returned.

"There, we should have no further interruptions." She picked up the soup tureen and set it before Parker. "Lentil, I hope you like."

"Lentil soup doesn't put meat on your bones or a fire in your belly, but I guess it'll be good enough," Parker answered and grabbed the ladle.

The next hour was perhaps the most unpleasant one of Lord Livingston's life. Not only were Parker's table manners atrocious, but he carped about everything.

The soup wasn't hearty enough. The ham was insufficient. The potatoes not hot enough. The vegetables stringy. The cake dry. In short, Parker seemed to like nothing about a meal that he polished off, down to the last crumb. To make matters worse, Lord Livingston had to fetch another whiskey for Parker in the middle of the meal. Had not Lord and Lady Livingston also needed more, Lord Livingston might have told Mr. Parker where to get off. Instead, Lord Livingston reminded himself of his charitable duty and tried to smile. At the end of the meal, Lady Livingston complained of a headache and went to bed. Lord Livingston sent Parker to the Library. Clearing the table didn't take Lord Livingston long. Parker had left no food, and the staff would no doubt come the next day to set everything to rights.

When Lord Livingston went to the library, he found Parker pouring himself a drink from the priciest bottle of Scotch in the manor. It was all Lord Livingston could do to keep from tossing Parker out on his ear.

"I got to hand it to ya," Parker said. "Ya got a dandy place here."

"Yes, well, I'm afraid we're done for the night."

Parker winked.

"I got ya. I'm off."

Lord Livingston watched Parker leave, glass in hand. Lord Livingston didn't hesitate. He grabbed the bottle of Scotch and carried it to the kitchen. The door to the kitchen had a lock, a throwback to the age when they feared for the silver. Lord Livingston made certain to lock the door before he retired.

Lady Livingston did indeed have a headache, and she had retired for the night after taking a sleep aid. Lord Livingston knew the pill would keep Lady Livingston in bed for the night, which suited him. He was still a bit riled by Parker. The man was insufferable. Lord Livingston considered taking a sleep aid but decided against it. He might need all his wits with Parker in the house. For Lord Livingston, morning light could not come soon enough.

The commotion began with the dog. The whining and scratching led Lord Livingston to believe the little beggar needed relief. But as Lord Livingston opened the door, he heard the noise from below. Something was amiss, and that something probably had a name — Parker. But if it didn't, Lord Livingston was not one to be caught unawares. He retrieved his revolver from the nightstand and left the room.

Lord Livingston could scarcely believe his eyes. Standing by the kitchen door, trying to pry it open, was Parker. His bag was at his feet.

"What in thunder do you think you're doing?" Lord Livingston demanded.

Parker turned, and his red face told Lord Livingston that his house guest had found the not-so-pricey whiskey.

"I dropped me kit," Parker said.

"It's right there." Lord Livingston pointed at the bag.

"That's me bag, not me kit."

"I don't give a damn what it is. You didn't leave anything in the kitchen."

"Ya don't understand."

"I understand that you have worn out your welcome. You are to leave the premises immediately."

"That's daft. It's not fit outside."

"I no longer care about the elements," Lord Livingston fumed. "You ate my food, drank my best whiskey, and now you're trying to steal. I should have you thrown in jail or shot. Now, march, Mr. Parker."

"Ya—"

"MARCH!"

Lord Livingston escorted Parker to the entry. There, he watched the smelly man put on his ragged coat. Whatever good intention Lord Livingston had conjured up, it was now lost. All he could think about was getting rid of Mr. Parker.

"If ya kick me out," Parker said. "I swear by all that's holy or unholy, that ya will never enjoy another happy Christmas in this place."

"Be gone."

"Hear me? I CURSE YA AND YA FAMILY FOR ALL ETERNITY!"

Lord Livingston waved the pistol. "You have five seconds before I shoot you. And I assure you that the police will believe whatever story I give them."

Parker's scowl almost frightened Lord Livingston, but he was not to be intimidated. He didn't have to count. Parker opened the door, wrapped himself in his coat and walked into the snow and wind. Lord Livingston watched until the ill-tempered man disappeared. Then, shivering at the frightful cold, Lord Livingston closed and locked the door. Whatever else happened, Mr. Parker was not coming back. Lord Livingston spent the night in the library, sipping whiskey between short naps. He was more than a bit surly in the morning.

Lord Livingston was on his third cup of tea when the maid arrived with the news.

A man, a vagrant, had been found in the snow halfway between the manor and the town. A stranger, no one knew who it was, or how he had managed to get where he fell and froze. The snow covered whatever tracks he might have made. It was as if he had been dropped from heaven.

Lord Livingston thought he knew who the man was, but he was not about to offer his certain knowledge that the dead man was no angel. When he informed Lady Livingston of the death, he made her promise to keep quiet also. There was no advantage in identifying the man. And indeed, by Christmas Eve, Lord Livingston had forgotten all about Mr. Parker. When the little terrier fell through the ice on the pond and drowned, Lord Livingston thought of it as an unlucky happenstance.

When he and Lady Livingston returned from church on Christmas day and found a window open and several pipes leaking from being frozen, he blamed the help. When the high-pitched keening began Christmas night, he blamed the shut down plumbing. It was the worst Christmas he and Lady Livingston had ever experienced.

And it seemed positively balmy compared to Christmas the next year.

The year after that, Lord and Lady Livingston took to spending the week before Christmas and right up to the 1st day of January in the new year in Europe, well away from the manor.

Chapter One

"Have I ever let you down?"

Zelda looked across the table at Jeremy and rolled her eyes. "Do I have to remind you?"

"The music festival doesn't count."

"Why doesn't the music festival count, as if I need that to make my case."

Jeremy smiled, and Zelda had to admit that when Jeremy smiled, he was exceedingly handsome, actor handsome. Since he was an actor, it seemed to be just another part of his persona.

"The music festival doesn't count because I got the call from the Beeb."

"That grants you immunity how?"

"The Beeb trumps the music festival. Everyone knows that."

"The Beeb called you to get Rodney's number, not to offer you a job."

"How was I to know that?" Jeremy went into character. Something she had seen him do a dozen times. "After all, I do have a certain following."

"You were a minor character in a series that lasted exactly three episodes. I wouldn't say you have a following. And even if you did, that's no reason to leave a friend in the lurch."

"Lurch? Were you performing?"

Zelda hated it when Jeremy projected his fears and problems onto others.

"You knew I wasn't performing, but I was introducing acts. You promised to help."

"OK, OK, I'll grant you the music festival then. But trust me, I'll be there for Christmas."

"Christmas Eve, Jeremy, Christmas Eve. The film crew will be there Christmas Eve, and they expect to see you and me and the others I've recruited. If they don't see us, well, that would be a very bad thing."

Jeremy sipped his latte and looked over Zelda's shoulder. She knew what he was doing. He had spotted some other handsome man who just might be the least little bit gay. Jeremy didn't hide his preferences. He flirted shamelessly with any attractive man he could find.

"Look here," Zelda and pointed to her eyes. "You can chase those trousers later. I want you to promise on your dead mother's grave that you'll come."

"My mother isn't dead. Well, not in that way. She doesn't really care for my choice of careers or lovers, but that makes no difference. I'll be there. By the way, why is this a big deal?"

"It's a big deal because TV watchers are always interested in the peerage."

"I'm not."

"Of course you are. You watch every royal wedding from start to finish."

"Those are the royals, not the peerage."

"Don't quibble. This is the first time in twenty-five years that the manor will be used at Christmas. It's a big deal. But the producers aren't just looking at Christmas. There's a series in the wind."

"And a role for you, correct?"

"Perhaps."

Jeremy leaned forward, as if conspiring. "What did they offer? Upstairs maid? Downstairs maid? Scullery wench?"

"You're mad."

"You'd make a winsome scullery wench. I mean, you have fantastic boobs. Let you show a little cleavage, and the show will take off."

"I take it back. You're not mad. You're bonkers. Maybe you shouldn't come on Christmas Eve."

"Hah! Try to keep me away. I'll be there with fairy bells on, and if you think I don't own a pair, you're kidding yourself."

Zelda laughed. No matter what, Jeremy always made her laugh, and that hadn't always been easy.

"Tell me," Jeremy said. "Why did your grands leave you the manor to begin with?"

"Because they wanted to keep it in the family. They knew that if they left it to my mother, she would sell it before the will had been read. Not that it might not come to that. If the producer decides on another manor, then, well, it will go to auction. I have put everything I have into reviving the manor. If Christmas goes well, then the series might take off. And believe, me, if that happens, I'll be happy to be the scullery maid, wearing whatever they want me to wear." Zelda looked at her watch. "I have to go." She stood. "If you don't show, Jeremy, I'm going to tell Rodney that you had a date with a real woman, not one of those shemales you hang with."

"That's low, Zelda, low. But he might just buy it. Now go, go, before I change my mind."

"Christmas Eve," Zelda said one last time, and turned away.

On her way across London, Zelda did review her coming ten days. She would move to the manor and attend to any details that had escaped notice. She would live there through the Christmas holidays, and with luck, she would put on a convincing show. When the producers reviewed the film crew footage, they would agree that the Livingston Manor was perfect for the next series about how the better half lived.

Not that Zelda had ever lived as most people supposed. Middle class for the most part. It wasn't her name or peerage family tree that got her into acting. It was her beauty and her hard work. Like every other actor she knew, she had developed the hide of a rhino.

She had reached the point where no one, no matter how mean, could hurt her. She considered herself tough. That was what she needed to be.

$\sim \sim \sim \sim \sim$

Natalia smiled and pulled her shawl closer. Natalia's office was cold, far colder than it needed to be. Zelda sat on her hands, half expecting her breath to turn white when she exhaled. It didn't, but that was small comfort.

"They gave me this office because they hate me," Natalia groused. "But I'll not give them any satisfaction by complaining. I'll be damned before I do that. They think I'm weak because I'm a woman."

Zelda smiled and waited. With Natalia, Zelda always walked on pins and needles. Natalia was shepherding the manor series through the bureaucratic maze that controlled the budget. Natalia had been the one to arrange for the film crew.

In a way, Natalia controlled Zelda's future. If the series took off, Zelda would be able to pay off the loan she had procured to rehab the manor.

That fuelled Zelda's smile and her every nod of agreement.

"Tell me we're all set," Natalia said. "All the decorations in place?"

"Every tree, candle, Santa, and elf," Zelda answered. "I hired the best decorators in London, the people who do sets for the Beeb. It wasn't easy, as the manor only came to me a month ago. You have no idea what's it's like to start from scratch. My grands had tossed everything that anything to do with Christmas, but don't fret, we're ready to go."

"Good. You'll be there, with Desert Devon?"

17

"Devon is on set in Africa, and he'll try to be home by Christmas Eve. He'll certainly make Christmas Day. Why can't England have a decent desert? Anyway, there will be plenty of guests at the party. I promise you some lively footage to review."

"Excellent. If I have the time, I'll stop by. But don't expect me. The day before Christmas is an absolute nightmare. My partner always complains if I'm not there to roll out the dough or something. Frankly, I don't care for cooking. Just hand me a bottle of wine and sit me at the table."

"I'm no cook either," Zelda said. "If you come, I promise you the biggest glass of wine ever."

"Now that is what I like to hear. Damn, it's cold. You'd better go. Your lips are turning blue."

The last person Zelda needed to see before she left for the manor was her mother. Their relationship had been strained by the grands decision to skip a generation and will the manor house to Zelda. By all rights, Zelda's mother should have received the house no matter what she intended to do with it. Zelda wanted to mend their rift, and perhaps more importantly, she wanted to make sure that her mother wouldn't show up on Christmas Eve and ruin the shoot. That would be a disaster.

Zelda's mother cut the apple in half and handed a half to her daughter.

"You don't eat enough," Zelda's mother said.

"I eat plenty," Zelda said. "How are you doing?"

"I'm fine, but that's not what you want to know. You want to know if I intend to show up Christmas Eve."

"Mother, you know what this is all about. Can I ask you to wait till Christmas Day? Is that too much to ask?"

"I know you think you know everything you need to know, but let me assure you, you don't. Haven't you ever wondered why your grandparents stopped celebrating Christmas at the manor?"

"I was three when they stopped. I don't remember much."

"Well, let me clue you in or something. The last few years they hosted Christmas, they had horrible luck. I mean, horrible luck. Things happened that shouldn't have happened, and while my mother and father never explained everything, it wasn't just the list of problems and accidents. Something scared them, scared them in a way they would not share. It scared them to the point where they stopped hosting Christmas."

"I don't get it," Zelda said. "Why Christmas? They lived there all the other months of the year, didn't they?"

"That always stumped me too. What was it about Christmas that made a difference? But no matter. You, my dear, have to be exceedingly careful. I know, I know you won't believe. It's all about undotted I's and uncrossed T's. But there are things out there no one can explain. Remember that. It's not all B follows A."

"I've had the manor checked from top to bottom. Trust me, trust my bank account. Everything is working just fine. I expect no problems. That said, can I depend on you to wait till Christmas Day?"

"Absolutely. And Zelda, you can come here any time you want during the Yuletide season."

"Why would I do that?"

"Why did your grands stop hosting Christmas?"

Zelda didn't answer. She didn't need to. She would be snug and safe and waiting for Santa to drop down the chimney and leave presents. A successful Christmas Eve filming would suit her just fine.

Zelda had almost reached her flat when her phone rang. The name was familiar, but why would the lawyer who had handled the grands' estate want to talk to her now?

Chapter Two

She answered and agreed to meet the lawyer in a pub halfway between her flat and his office. She told him to order her a pint, since he would probably get there first. He told her he would order fish and chips too. She didn't have the heart to tell him that she was not all that fond of fish and chips. Of course, she was pretty sure that the lawyer would finish the dish no matter what she did or didn't eat.

Zelda like pubs, but this was her second one in a few hours. She found the lawyer sitting at a small table in the middle of a quickly filling room. He was digging into the fish and chips, which suited her. She grabbed her pint and smiled.

"This is absolutely the best fish in London," the lawyer said. "I come every chance I get. My wife believes it's all about meeting clients, and it is, it is, but I love to eat while I'm here."

"No one can fault you for eating while you wait."

"And it's a legitimate expense. If I do business while I eat, well, let's say it's a win-win."

"And what business do you have with me tonight?"

Zelda looked around the pub, and she knew she had to thank the lawyer for his cover. As long as he was there, she wouldn't have to worry about the blokes giving her the once-over. Without the lawyer, Zelda would soon have to field the overtures of the blokes who would offer a beer and something clever like… "haven't I seen you on the Beeb?"

"I have a letter for you," the lawyer said and licked his fingers.

Zelda frowned. The last thing she wanted was the lawyer's germs on her letter. Why did people think that licking their fingers was all right?

The lawyer surprised Zelda by using his paper napkin to pull an envelope out of his briefcase. With a smile, he pushed the envelope across the table.

"What is this?" Zelda

"A letter from your grandparents."

"And why am I getting it now?"

"Because that was the stipulation of the will. Today is exactly seven days before Christmas. You get the letter."

"What does it say?"

He stared at her before he laughed.

"I know lawyers are thought of as patently dishonest, but in most cases, we're more honest than most. Of course, when there's a lot of money at stake…"

He grinned.

"No hints?"

"None. They absolutely refused to offer any hints. That may have been because she seemed a bit addled, but your grandfather was still sharp. And that's all I can tell you."

Zelda sipped her pint.

She was tempted to open the envelope and read the letter right then, but she told herself to wait. She had the idea that the lawyer was hoping she would reveal the contents of the letter. Zelda wasn't about to sate the lawyer's appetite for information. Instead, she stood.

"Thank you very much," she said and walked away.

"You're welcome," he called after her.

During the trek back to her flat, Zelda wondered about the letter. To her reckoning, her grands had never been ones to protect secrets and play games.

They had generally insisted on straightforward communications and relationships. Yet, they had given their lawyer a letter which had to be presented precisely seven days before Christmas.

Beyond odd, it was strange, the kind of strange that people found disturbing. Of course, it might be nothing but some sort of joke. You know, we forgot to tell you... there is no Santa Claus. But the grands weren't practical jokers either.

What was in the letter?

In the privacy of her flat, Zelda could no longer hold back the curiosity. She opened the envelope, pulled out a letter and spread it on the table.

Dearest Zelda,

If all has gone as planned, you are the owner of Livingston Manor. Congratulations. You are now part of history. The manor has stood tall and proud since the age of Victoria, and we have always taken great pride in our history. More, we have always looked with hope and great expectations at the future. We put our faith in you. We know you will carry on the great Livingston name.

Zelda paused for a moment. While she shared the grands feelings, she knew that the letter wasn't some kind of cheer thing. The grands weren't like that. They had something else to share.

We have debated long and hard about sharing a tale with you. Your grandmother wishes to warn you, and I have come to agree with her. We hope the Yuletide curse will die with us, but we cannot be certain. We had thought the curse would have worn off by now, but we are not willing to test our faith. We realize that this talk of a curse is disconcerting. No one wishes to hear that their home carries the stigma of bad luck. So, here is our story, minus the details that now embarrass us.

More than 25 years ago, I picked up a vagrant in the middle of a snow storm. I shouldn't have, but it was a week before Christmas, and the night was deadly. To be concise, we welcomed a ne'er-do-well to our house and our table. We were met with treachery. When I drove the scoundrel back into the storm, he cursed our house. We would never have a pleasant Christmas again, not in that house. We, of course, didn't believe it. Curses are always tommyrot.

But the man died during the night.

We regretted the death, but still paid no attention to the curse. But starting with that Christmas, unexpected and unexplained accidents happened in the manor. They stopped the day after Christmas, but for the week before Christmas, the house was, well, unreliable, despite our best efforts.

After several years, we decided to forego the Christmas holidays and spend our time somewhere else instead. The decision amazed those closest to us, but it was necessary.

We're certain that at this point, you are wondering why we bothered with this letter. Good question. We felt we would be remiss if we did not share our story and our concern. The accidents we endured were not pranks. That is why we seek to inform you. You may be in danger... although we pray not.

This is far longer than we had hoped to make it, but we trust you will heed our words. We will be watching from heaven, and we hope to see you lock up the manor and spend the Yuletide season in Spain or France or anywhere else away.

Your loving grandparents,

Lord and Lady Livingston

Zelda put the letter down. Her first response was to discount the letter as an exercise of dementia or comedy. 'Cursed?' What kind of babble was that? Curses were for old books and cartoons. It was silly and she couldn't possibly heed the letter.

She had invested her near future in the manor, and in a manor Christmas. Putting any stock in the letter would be the response of an idiot, and she was certain that her grandparents did not expect her to act like a dummy.

No, at the end, when her grandparents had faced the end and lost the ability to think, then, only then, had they felt the need to tell a story to try to scare their grandchild. No, she couldn't put any stock in a Yuletide curse. Not even a witch would be so silly. Zelda shook her head and headed for bed, leaving the letter on the table. By the time she reached her bedroom, she had pretty much forgotten the exact words in the letter. It didn't matter. She had a holiday manor to sell to a particular producer.

The next morning, Zelda placed her packed bags in her small car and headed away from London. There were six days before Christmas, five before Christmas Eve. She had five days to make sure that the manor would be as perfect as she could make it. Five days. She thought it should be enough. After all, she had already paid for the decorating. All the house needed was her artistic touch.

As Zelda drove into the horseshoe drive which led to the manor, she smiled. Garlands and lights decorated the front, and she spotted more lights in the shrubbery. There was a Santa and a fat snowman on the lawn, along with as sleigh and those iconic eight, tiny reindeer. It looked exactly as she wanted it to look. At night, it would look just right, neither too much nor too little, just right for a Christmas display.

Inside the manor, the decorations continued. Zelda carried her bags past the Christmas tree in the entry and the big tree in the great hall and the little tree at the top of the stairs.

If Natalia was looking for a perfect house for filming, she would find it — in exactly five days. Zelda wanted to laugh. In the master bedroom, there was yet one more tree with an angel on top. Angels were good luck, weren't they? Zelda knew she needed all the luck she could get.

As she unpacked, she remembered her grandparents' letter. As far as Zelda could see, the letter was some kind of misguided sham. She assumed the grands meant well, but they were clearly a bit addled when they composed the letter. So be it.

She spent the rest of the day going through the manor, room by room. She checked the decorations, the lights, the windows. She checked the fireplaces — of which there were far too many. She checked the kitchen. She even checked the basement and the furnace that fed the central air system. It was December, and that meant it might get cold. She couldn't rely on the guests to provide all the heat.

By dinner time, she was satisfied that all was well in the manor. Then, she drove to into town for a pint and some food. The idea of a small pub on the outskirts suited her just fine. Something tiny and out of the way would protected her from the blokes in the town. By the time she returned to the manor, she was mellow and hopeful.

The outside decorations looked positively perfect all lit up. It was ready for a country Christmas. Locking the door behind her, she smiled as she headed for the master bedroom.

She passed all those decorations she had checked earlier. They were alight also, all plugged into timers which worked automatically. It was a fantasy house. How could Natalia not fall in love with it?

Zelda slipped into bed and looked at the Christmas tree and its lucky angel. It provided the only light in the room, and it warmed her far more than the goose-down comforter on the bed. She could feel success with her fingertips. Everything was going well. She had only to keep doing what she was doing. In her heart, she was certain that the grands were looking down and smiling. Livingston Manor was going to live for one more generation. She fell asleep with that thought.

When the alarm sounded, Zelda looked at her bedside clock... 12:01.

Chapter Three

Zelda was out of the bed in a flash, but in the dark, she hardly knew which way to turn. This wasn't her flat. It was the manor house. She stumbled across the room and found the light switch. As light flooded the room, she jerked open the door.

The alarm was louder.

She knew fire alarms had been added to the house at some point in the past. Any renovation had to include alarms in order to get approved by the local council. But Zelda had no idea which alarm had been triggered, or what had caused the alarm to go off. She immediately thought of the kitchen. Didn't most fires start in the kitchen? She hadn't cooked anything or turned on any burners, mostly because she didn't want to create any kind of mess. That would come on Christmas Eve.

As she hurried through the manor, she turned on lights, happy that she had checked those earlier. At least, the electricity hadn't been affected. At the bottom of the stairs, the alarm was louder still, and she was certain it was in the kitchen. She hurried to the kitchen door and stopped.

The door was locked.

Locked?

She pushed harder, as if the door were stuck. But it wasn't. It was clearly locked, and she didn't remember locking it. She knew there was a lock on the door, but she wasn't aware of a key. There had to be one. Where was it?

The blaring alarm didn't help Zelda think. She knew there was a ring of keys somewhere. She had seen them... where? She closed her eyes and tried to picture where she had seen them. She was pretty sure they weren't in the kitchen. She hoped they weren't in the kitchen, because if that were the case... well, she didn't want to face that problem.

She couldn't remember.

She stepped back, wanting to scream. There had to be a solution. Even if she couldn't remember where the keyring was, there had to be a solution.

She simply had to think, but thinking was difficult with the alarm filling the house with noise.

Was the alarm hooked into the local fire brigade?

She hadn't thought of that. If the fire trucks were on the way, there was a very good chance that some fireman with an axe would chop right through the kitchen door. That would be a disaster. The house was perfect.

A bunch of tromping firemen would destroy... everything. She wouldn't have enough time or money to put the house back to rights. No, no, no, she couldn't afford an invasion by the fire people. She had to find another way.

And then the idea hit her. She had a way in. She turned and ran back the way she had come. In the bedroom, she grabbed the keys from her purse. She knew that a single key unlocked both front and back doors. She ran down the stairs and out the front door. The air seemed colder than it had been earlier, but she paid it no mind. She ran around the dark house as fast as she could. When she reached the back door, she thought she heard a siren.

Siren?

It wasn't a siren, it was Armageddon. She had to hurry. She unlocked the kitchen door, which gave her hope.

Bursting into the kitchen, she flicked on the light and spotted the offending alarm. As far as she could see, there was no smoke or fire or anything.

It was as if the alarm had gone off by itself, which made no sense. She sniffed the air. She didn't smell smoke or anything burning. Why?

It didn't matter.

She grabbed a chair from the kitchen table and dragged it across the room to the alarm which was too far up the wall for her to reach. She jumped onto the chair and punched the reset button.

Nothing happened.

That was crazy. Something had to happen. She punched the button half a dozen times before she realized that the button wasn't working, which made sense. If the alarm had malfunctioned, then it had malfunctioned.

Up close, the sound was deafening. Was there a siren outside? Zelda began to panic. She had to kill the alarm and kill it fast. She fiddled with the cover and after a minute, managed to remove it. A 10-volt battery was in a socket, and she fought it for another minute before she managed to remove it.

The alarm didn't quit.

Tears formed in Zelda's eyes. What was happening? She stared at the alarm, and she noticed a catch. What did that mean?

She undid the catch, and the alarm fell off the wall, dragging two wires with it. She grabbed the alarm, and on the back was a switch. Not knowing what else to do, she flipped it.

The alarm quit.

Ears ringing, Zelda blinked away the tears and let the alarm dangle. Breathing far too hard, she stepped off the chair and held it onto it. Her body shook. Her brain seemed befogged. She looked up at the alarm and wondered just how it went off. She was certain she could get it repaired before Christmas Eve, but she needed to know what had set off the alarm. The last thing she needed was an alarm chasing people out of the manor on Christmas Eve.

Firemen.

The image of helmeted firemen running through her house scared Zelda to action. She ran to the door and shoved.

The door didn't move.

The door was still locked, and there was nothing but another keyhole on this side.

Without a key, there was no way to unlock the door. Cursing under her breath, she turned and hustled out the back door. She didn't bother locking it. Panting, she ran back the way she had come.

Around the house, she listened for the sirens. Reaching the front, she stopped and stared toward the town. Her breath coming out white, she listened.

No sirens.

She didn't know whether to be happy or upset. No firemen meant the manor house wouldn't be destroyed in the name of being saved. It also meant that the alarm system was not hooked into any other system. If it did catch fire, no one would know unless they happened past and heard the alarm. Was that the way it was supposed to work? She knew it wasn't.

What good was an alarm system that didn't contact the authorities? She told herself she would have to explore a connection. Didn't they have systems that used the Internet to report fires? She hoped so. That might make it infinitely easier.

For a moment, she considered going around to lock the back door, but that hardly seemed worth the trouble. If someone did happen into the kitchen, he would be stymied by the locked kitchen door. The rest of the house was off limits.

Feeling half good about that, Zelda went inside, locked the door, and returned to her bed.

Fatigue washed over her. The last thing she needed was a midnight adventure. She told her brain to remember about the electrician — not that she was going to forget.

As her eyes closed, she breathed a sigh of relief. She had dodged two problems, fire and firemen. Of course, if the kitchen caught on fire...

She didn't pursue that thought. The kitchen, the manor was safe. She had to believe that even as sleep took her.

When Zelda woke, she thought it was early, very early. The gloom was unexpected. She looked at the clock and realized she had slept past her usual wake up time. That was to be expected after the night she had endured. A fire alarm? She would have never believed that if someone had told her. Sliding out of bed, Zelda yawned as she shuffled to the bathroom. She brushed and rinsed her teeth, and when she straightened, she spotted the man in the mirror.

Chapter Four

Zelda whirled, toothbrush held with intent to harm.

The doorway was empty. For a moment, she wondered if perhaps she had imagined the man. But had she? And if she hadn't, that meant there was a man loose in her house! But did she really see that? Perhaps she had imagined it. Yes, that was it, that would be best, if she'd just imagined it, but yet, she had to check, just to make sure.

Anger and fear mixed within her as she walked into the bedroom. If there was someone around, she would fully expect to spot the man scarpering out the bedroom door, and If the door was open, she knew the fear would gain the upper hand. Zelda sighed in relief, the door was closed. Nonetheless she gingerly pushed the door open — just to make sure.

There was no one in the room. Was that better or worse? Zelda knew what she had *thought* she'd seen. She couldn't be that barmy could she? What... if he hadn't left? A fresh swirl of fear stirred in the pit of her stomach. She had to know. If there was someone, she couldn't just ignore it.

There was a minute of indecision before she walked to the closet, and pulled it open in a fierce movement. but no man faced her. Feeling emboldened Zelda moved off and carefully checked the adjacent makeup room, smaller with its lighted mirror.

No one.

Zelda moved back to the bed and look all around. The French doors leading to the balcony were locked tight. She had just checked all of the rooms. If there was a man, he would have had to have the speed of gazelle to get out of the bedroom before she left the bathroom. So, she was certain that the man hadn't gone that way.

If there had been a man at all.

She bit her lip and worked through her memory. She had seen a man in the mirror, a rather scruffy man with a sort of leer. But apparently, he had not been there at all. Her mind had conjured up the image. She had to accept it, and really that didn't surprise her after her battle with the fire alarm. She was tired, rattled.

She had never been given to visions in the past, but the mind was a funny thing. She was all alone in a big house. Maybe, she simply wanted, in some unconscious way, to find a cause for the fire alarm. An unannounced man might fill that bill.

She looked around one more time before she decided that she had experienced some kind of episode. Now that she was fully awake, she knew it was just her imagination. She was alone.

Happily, she grabbed her phone. It was time for tea.

Zelda had reached the kitchen door before she remembered that it was locked. She was about to return for her keys when she decided to push the door anyway. To her surprise, the door swung open.

And Zelda shivered.

She knew that the door was supposed to be locked. She had left it that way the night before. She distinctly remembered trying the door from both sides, and it had been locked in both directions. Yet, it now was unlocked. Which meant...

That someone was in the house?

For a moment, her mind failed to process the thought. If someone had unlocked the door, then that someone had found the keyring. With the keyring, that someone could lock and unlock any number of doors in the manor.

Zelda stopped still and contemplated. An uncomfortable lump rose in her throat. She had to find the person who had unlocked the kitchen door — a man with a scruffy beard perhaps — and, she had to find the keyring. Without the keyring, that someone would be able to come and go at will. A cold fear echoed through her mind. This was not supposed to happen. Not knowing what else to do, she tapped her phone. Perhaps, Devon would know.

Devon picked up on the first ring.

"I was hoping you'd call."

"I've been busy at the manor, checking everything is ready."

"Good news. I should be back Christmas Eve, late of course. Keep the party going for me."

"If there is a party."

"I detect a problem?

"I... ahhh, I'm seeing things. I mean, I hope I am.

"Come again?"

Zelda outlined the faulty alarm, and the man in the bedroom, and the unlocked kitchen door. But as she spoke, she realized how odd that would sound to someone a thousand miles away.

"Perhaps, you should leave. I mean, if there's a stranger in the place."

"No, no, it's just my mind playing tricks. The party... my mother... I'm under a lot of stress. I just need a cup of tea."

Zelda chatted for another minute before Devon told her they were about to shoot a scene. Their good-byes were quick. And while Zelda felt better, she was still not entirely sure about the stranger — if there was a stranger.

Carefully, she pushed open the door and stepped into the kitchen.

The kitchen was empty. Zelda was glad of that, and the first thing she did was march to the back door, and lock it. Feeling better, she glanced up at the dangling fire alarm. That was comforting also, as it proved she had not dreamed the episode. From a cabinet drawer, she pulled a long, sharp knife. She didn't think that she would need it, but it was better to have it anyway. With that, she set about her search. She tackled the pantry first.

The pantry was devoid of life, its shelves holding nothing but some tins. Zelda hadn't bothered laying a stock of food.

The Christmas Eve party was being catered, and she had planned to eat out in an effort to avoid messes.

Satisfied, she next went to the basement door. She wasn't pleased about having to explore the basement, but she did not wish to leave a stone unturned. But before she tried the basement, she pulled a chair and put it by the door. If someone entered, they would move the chair and hopefully alert her. With her back covered, she slowly descended into the basement.

The basement was mostly one big room. There was a door at the far end that Zelda knew she would have to open, and there was a wooden shaft on one wall. If she remembered correctly the shaft was the dumbwaiter which had gone out of use long before the manor ceased to host Christmas parties. The rest of the room was dank and smelled of mildew.

She supposed that every house, if it existed for long enough, would become the abode of mould and mildew. When the rest of the world had burned up in some epic conflagration, mould and mildew would rule. But there was no man, and there was no keyring. Feeling more than a bit antsy, she marched to the door and with a deep breath, pulled it open.

Coal bin. Behind the door was the coal bin, minus the coal. It was empty too, and as she held the door open, an odour washed over her. It was a decidedly foul odour that made her pinch shut her nose and slam the door closed. She backed away from the door, hoping the stench didn't somehow leak out. It was awful. Shaking her head, trying to fling off the smell, Zelda reminded herself that she would need to bring in some experts in order to banish the odour permanently.

In the kitchen, Zelda was feeling a bit proud of herself. The chair by the door was exactly as she had placed it. Only a ghost could have passed the chair. There was still no sign of her keyring, but she hoped it would turn up directly. She didn't want the keyring to be lost. She moved the chair and passed through the door.

On the other side, Zelda stopped. She needed a way to ensure that if someone was in the house, that someone wouldn't slip into the kitchen when her back was turned. She had the feeling that her efforts were overkill. After all she was just behaving like a complete ditz. Surely there wasn't anyone but herself in the house. Yet the nagging feeling that danced inside her head told her to be as certain as certain can be.

Since she couldn't lock the door, she decided on the chair trick. She retrieved a heavy chair from the dining room and set it against the kitchen door. She carefully marked the exact position.

If someone moved the chair to get into the kitchen, then they couldn't put it back in *exactly* the same position, right? Still, she wanted to be sure the chair wasn't moved. Satisfied, she set about checking the ground floor.

Her first mission was the front door. She made sure it was locked. Feeling safer, and half assured, she passed from room to room. The great hall, the entry, the dining room, where she checked the French doors, the study, and the library. She was pleased to find the keyring on the desk in the library. She checked closets and opened any door she noticed. She found no one. No man with a scruffy beard, no animal, nothing. Smiling at her thoroughness, she felt a moment of pride. She was making progress.

Telling herself that she was halfway finished, she went up the stairs and checked the bedrooms. Every bedroom had an old-fashioned lock that she made sure to lock before moving on to the next room. Half an hour later, she had gone through every room, and she had found nothing. That seemed fantastic. She felt lighter than ever. She pulled out her phone and searched for an electrician. She found one who could come out immediately, which was perfect. Then, she left the second floor and returned to the kitchen.

But she didn't reach the kitchen. She stopped short. The chair she had left guarding the door had been moved.

The chill that ran up her spine didn't stop at her neck. It ran to the top of her head. For a moment, her knees shook so badly, she thought that she might topple over. It was all she could do to keep from racing out of the house.

She still had the knife, and that gave her a bit more confidence. She pulled up her courage and pushed against the door.

It didn't budge.

She pulled the keyring from her pocket. How could the chair be moved and the door locked? If that were true, then whoever had locked the door was... behind her.

Zelda spun, and out of the corner of her eye, she spotted something, something black, a man? Whatever it was, it was headed for the dining room. She didn't hesitate.

"HELLO! HEY! HEY! Zelda called and ran after the figure.

She entered the dining room seconds after the figure, and even as she entered, she knew that the room was empty.

Holding the knife high, she faced the table and chairs and china cabinet, all mute and unyielding.

"Where are you?" she called. "I know you're in here!"

No one answered.

She bent down and looked under the long table.

Nothing.

"Come on! I'm going to find you. Save me the trouble. Show yourself!"

The laugh made the hair on her arms stand up in fear. Because the laugh came from all around her.

Chapter Five

It was as if speakers in every corner bombarded her with the laugh at the same time. It was as if the laugh had penetrated her skin. It sort of echoed through her body, filling her with a fear she had never known before. What the bloody hell was that? She shivered and turned in a full circle as the laugh died. Zelda had worked on the sets of several horror movies, and she had heard her share of wicked laughs, but she had never heard anything half as scary as the laugh in the dining room.

One slow step at a time, waiting for the next awful laugh, Zelda backed out of the dining room.

A loud ominous chime rang through the air and Zelda jumped for a second time. Almost peeing herself, Zelda stopped and grabbed at the wall. It sounded again. A huge relief flooded through her. She knew what it was.

The doorbell. It had surprised her, but at least she wasn't scared half to death. Gratefully, she turned from the dining room and the person she couldn't find, and fairly ran for the front door.

43

The man on the front step smiled. He explained that he was the electrician she had called. To Zelda, he was a godsend, and not just for the wiring. She was thrilled to have someone else in the manor with her. There was safety in numbers, wasn't there?

"Follow me," she said.

Zelda led the electrician, whose name was Tod, into the kitchen, where she pointed at the dangling detector.

"You did a bloody good job on that," Tod said and put down his tool box.

"It wouldn't stop," she explained. "And it was after midnight, and well, I thought the firemen would be coming, and since the house is filled with breakables—"

"Right, you have a right million little goo-gaws around here."

"It's for a Christmas party."

"I figured as much, although I was little doubtful when I saw the Santa and the snowman.

"What do you mean?"

"I thought perhaps it was some sort of horror Christmas."

"What?"

"On the lawn. It's right good for horror."

"Excuse me."

Without another word, Zelda turned and hurried away. Passing through the rooms, Zelda ran Tod's words through her mind. Horror? Santa Claus? Snowman? What did he mean? In seconds, she was out the front door, and she instantly saw what Tod was talking about.

There on the lawn grinned Santa and the Snowman. The heads had been detached from the bodies, and while they had not been damaged — as far as she could see — they were definitely no longer in place. Vandalism? What yob had come by in the dark, in the middle of the night and decapitated her lawn decorations? She was suddenly incensed. She had poured blood, sweat, tears, and money into those decorations, and they had been mutilated. Her blood boiled. It wasn't right. It wasn't fair.

She picked up Santa's head and carefully replaced it on the body. The beard was dirty with a strand or two of grass, but she guessed it would look all right from a distance.

The snowman's top hat was a few steps away from the head proper, and it had sustained a definite dent.

Zelda popped out the dent and put the hat back on the head. Like Santa, she was able to put the head back on the snowman, but it was decidedly out of kilter. No matter what she did, the head leaned the wrong way. After a few tries, she decided the snowman would have to make do with a bad head and hat. Then, she hurried back into the manor. She had to call the bobbies.

By the time Zelda had finished with the police, who were not all that interested in vandalism, Tod had completed his work with the alarm.

"I couldn't find anything wrong with it," Tod said. "And I tested the wires and the breaker. They all tested clean. But I replaced the device anyway. Sometimes, that's the best you can do."

"And the rest of the alarm system?"

"As good as gold. Do you know you're not connected to the local station?"

"I was aware of that, and I think I'll connect soon."

"I can get that done for you."

"Not right now, but I'll let you know."

Zelda escorted Tod out the door and felt better, but she wasn't exactly sure why. Back in the house, she locked the front door and tried to remember what she had been doing when the doorbell rang. She had just heard the... laugh.

And she had been scared.

Zelda didn't know everything, but she knew she needed a cup of tea. Confusion clouded her mind. Locked doors, unlocked doors, moved chairs, unmoved chairs, midnight alarms, wicked laugh, she needed something to soothe her brain and allow her to think.

Tea, she needed tea.

She was on her second cup of tea when the call came. Natalia needed to meet for dinner. There was another producer that needed babysitting, and Natalia couldn't do it alone. Zelda was just the person who could keep the producer on board. Zelda didn't want to make the trip to London; she wouldn't be able to drive back to the manor until the morning.

That wasn't a real problem, since Zelda still had her flat in London. Yet, she wanted to be at the manor. If the alarm tripped again? If the vandals struck? Of course, if the producer caved, then there might not be a reason for a Christmas Eve party. No she had to go. Zelda killed the connection and was soon ready for the dinner.

The drive to London passed without incident and Zelda hardly noticed the landscape going by. She was on autopilot. As she drove, her brain listed the concerns roiling inside her head. There was the grands' letter that, while over the top, still came from people Zelda knew and admired. Then, there was the man that wasn't there, and her worry about her mind. And, of course, there was Devon. Just when she needed a helping hand, he was making a movie in some African desert. Without really thinking, she reached her destination, half wondering just how she had done it.

The dinner went as hoped. Zelda was at her charming best, and the producer laughed himself into agreeing to fund the pilot in Livingston Manor, at least for the time being. He would make certain to attend the Christmas Eve party to see exactly how the series could be filmed. Natalia waxed loquacious when she praised Zelda after the meal. But, for Zelda, the result was far from perfectly satisfying. She had to spend the night in her flat, which meant she couldn't protect the manor. Thus, her sleep was fitful and hardly resting. She woke early and left her flat after a single cup of tea. She had a sinking feeling in her tummy that told her things had not gone well during the night. As she drove up to the manor, her feeling became reality.

The vandals had struck.

The eight tiny reindeer had been rearranged, four staged over the other four, as if engaged in reindeer sex.

While Zelda admitted that the sight was humorous, it was not the effect she was seeking. She spent fifteen minutes returning the reindeer to their proper order, and she hoped reindeer duty wouldn't be her first task every morning. As she unlocked the door, she listened for an alarm.

Not hearing one, she smiled. At least, Tod, the electrician, had done his job. She closed the door behind her and shivered. The temperature inside the manor had dropped precipitously.

Rubbing her arms, teeth chattering, she hurried to the thermostat. Surely that hadn't busted too?

No, it had been turned off.

Off? The sinking sensation in her stomach pulled at her.

She turned on the system and wondered who had turned it off. It hadn't been her. She had been absent, and she didn't remember turning it off before she left. Pondering the puzzle, she walked to the kitchen for a cup of tea. Tea would help her think.

As the water heated, Zelda smacked her forehead. Of course, Tod had turned off the system while he was working on the alarm. It was simple. He'd simply forgotten to turn it back on. Nothing mysterious about that. She smiled at her cleverness — and with only one cup of tea.

Feeling good about herself, she almost overlooked the open door to the basement. She stared at the door because she knew full well that she had not left that door open. A chill ran down her spine. She remembered the man with the scruffy beard. She remembered the figure slipping around a corner. Those were not good memories, not good memories at all. She grabbed a knife from the drawer and faced the yawning blackness of the basement. She wished she didn't have to go down there, but she had no choice. At the top of the stairs, she flicked on the light, and she was gratified that the lights came on below. Checking out the basement in the dark wasn't something she wished to do.

Gripping the knife tight, she went down the steps slowly. She peered ahead into the room. She was near the bottom when she tripped.

Only, it didn't feel like a trip. It felt as if someone had grabbed her ankle and made her miss the step. She tumbled the last few steps, wondering who had made her fall. She, foolishly, held onto the knife as she slammed into the hard concrete.

She felt the burn of the cut as the knife sliced her arm. Yet, she didn't focus on the cut. Scrambling to her knees, she faced the steps and the person who had made her fall.

There was no one under the stairs. No one who had reached between the risers to grab her ankle. She could see perfectly well to the wall, and she was all alone. She shook afresh, half in fear, half with adrenaline. She was absolutely certain someone had grabbed her. And yet…

She glanced at her arm, at the wound which was bleeding profusely. She had missed the arteries, but she had managed to cut herself worse than she wanted to admit. Knowing that she had to do something about the cut, she struggled to her feet.

She still looked at the stairs. Someone had been there. Well, she thought someone had been there. But that couldn't be, because no one could simply disappear in a lighted, empty room. So, unless she was bonkers, she had clumsily fallen and cut her arm. Still with the knife, she started up the steps, looking down to make sure no one grabbed her ankle. She held the wounded arm aloft, hoping that would stem the bleeding. That hurt her shoulder. What the bloody hell? An injured shoulder to go along with the bloody arm? And she hadn't even searched the basement!

This day, with just three to go till Christmas Eve, was turning out to be a disaster.

In the kitchen, Zelda found an old towel and wrapped it around her arm. She searched the drawers for something to hold the towel in place.

She didn't want to fill her car with blood stains and needed to stop the flow. All she found was a small bungee cord with metal hooks. She wrapped the cord around the towel and made it tight before she engaged the hooks. While the cord did its intended job, the result looked like the work of some country bumpkin. And she felt like a bumpkin.

Grabbing her purse, she headed for the car, but not before she closed the basement door. As she drove for care, she wondered if she could blame the open door on Tod. Had he gone down to the basement? Of course, he had. Had he tripped her?

The hospital took an enormous amount of time to get through. The queue was improbably long, and the most pressing problems were handled first. Zelda would have thought that the week before Christmas would be light, as people were running around, buying those last-minute gifts. Instead, the waiting room was filled with a variety of burns, breaks, and chest pains. It was past lunch time before a young, female doctor undid the bungee cord and looked at Zelda's wound.

"How did you manage that?" the doctor asked.

"I fell down the basement steps while holding a knife," Zelda answered.

The doctor raised her eyebrows.

"And why did you have a knife in the first place? Giant mice?"

The doctor laughed, which didn't please Zelda in the least. She did not want to explain about the door Tod had forgotten to close, or the feeling of having her ankle grabbed, or even her painful shoulder.

"To tell the truth," Zelda lied. "There were some Christmas decorations taped up in a box, and I needed to cut the tape. Silly of me."

"Well, let this be a lesson. Use scissors next time and toss them away if you happen to trip."

"I'll remember to do that."

"Well, well, well," the doctor said as she examined the cut. "This seems to be closing nicely. I don't think you need stitches. Just some glue and a bandage should suffice."

"Glue?"

"Don't worry, it works better than stitches on a wound like this. You'll have minimal scarring."

"Why doesn't that reassure me?"

"Scissors next time?"

Zelda nodded.

"Next time."

On the drive back to the manor, Zelda stopped for the pain killer the doctor had recommended. The doctor had said that the pain killer had an added benefit. It would help her sleep. In her current state, Zelda could use some restful sleep.

As she pulled up to the manor, she checked out the lawn decorations. As far as she could see, the Santa and the snowman looked just fine, and the reindeer hadn't decided to repeat their rowdy behaviour.

Zelda's arm throbbed as she locked the front door behind her. There was a certain fear that dropped over her as she walked to the kitchen. She needed a cup, and she needed something to stem the pain. Her head was woozy, perhaps the 'glue' wasn't so innocuous after all. In the kitchen, she checked the basement door. It was safely closed. That pleased her. As the water heated, she found herself ravenous. She hadn't eaten all day, and the stint in hospital had sapped whatever reserve energy she had. So, she turned off the water and grabbed her purse. She thought about taking a pain pill, but that didn't make sense, not if it made her sleep. She locked the front door and turned to her car. She stared at the lawn decorations, and she wanted to cry.

Chapter Six

Santa no longer had his head. The snowman was headless too. The deer had been arranged in a circle, nose to tail, and that struck Zelda as not very festive. Several candles had been knocked over, and the sleigh itself had been tipped on its side.

She stared at the vandalism and wondered how it had occurred without her noticing? Looking in every direction she didn't spot a roving band of teens bent on destruction. She didn't see anyone, and yet, someone had caused the damage.

A sudden anger surged inside her. She would not stand for this. She dropped her purse and stormed across the lawn. Putting everything back in place, her arm hurting, her eyes watering, she fought the urge to scream. Who was doing this? If she knew, she would think about using the knife on them. It was such a waste. Did she need a guard dog or something? That might keep the vandals at bay. A good nip here and there might be the lesson those thugs needed. Snatching up her purse, Zelda jumped into her car. If the devils came back, she would contact the bobbies again.

The pub was but a quarter full. Zelda found a table at the rear and ordered a pint. When it arrived, she ordered food. She knew she shouldn't drink on an empty stomach, not if she was going to drive back to the manor. While she sipped and waited, she pulled out her phone to check on what was happening away from the manor. She had the usual messages from Jeremy and Natalia, and she wondered if those two could actually live without sending out a stream of rather useless messages. She answered several, deleted the rest, and hoped the ale would tamp down the pain in her arm.

"Excuse me."

Zelda looked up into perhaps the kindest face she had ever happened upon.

"My name is Martha," the woman said. "You own Livingston, don't you?"

"Yes, that is my pleasure now."

"Do you mind if I sit?"

"Not at all." Zelda had no idea what the woman wanted, but Martha looked utterly harmless.

Harmless was precisely what Zelda thought she needed at the moment. Well, she needed to be through with the Christmas Eve party also, but that was still days away.

"I want to thank you for bringing back the Christmas tradition," Martha said.

"I thought it would be fun," Zelda answered.

"Well, I can't tell you how I've missed it over the years. Before the 'incident', it was the best house party in the shire."

Martha looked to be twice Zelda's age — at least. The lines of age were deep and telling. Martha's watery blue eyes said more.

"I was too young to remember much," Zelda said. "Perhaps, you can give me some hints as to how to make the party authentic."

"Well, you must have the eggnog and figgy pudding."

"Figgy pudding?"

"The Lord and Lady always had a Dickens theme."

"I see."

Martha continued with her memories of the party, from the food to the drinks to the decorations. Zelda admitted to herself that her party was not going to mimic her grands' parties, and that didn't bother Zelda in the least. She was throwing a party for the present, not the past.

"Of course, you must take care with all the food. That was what caused the problem with your grands."

"The food?" Zelda asked.

"Oh, my, yes. In those days, the cook prepared everything, and it was all artfully and tastefully done. You can't have a good party without quality food. That was why the 'incident' was so mysterious. There had never been an issue of tainted food before."

Zelda leaned forward. She had never heard this story, perhaps because it was an 'incident'. No one liked to recount their mistakes.

"What was the tainted food?"

"Why the figgy pudding, of course. Not that people liked figgy pudding, but they always had some. And the 'problems' started shortly after eating. I confess I had my own 'issues' after I ate it too. And while no one actually died, there were several who went to hospital."

"That's awful, I had no idea."

"That was the last year, of course."

"What? I never heard about that."

"The year before was the tree fire. It happened after everyone had left. A short in the tree lights or something. Luckily, the dog barked a warning, or the entire manor might have burned to the ground."

"That's another story I have never heard," Zelda noted.

"Oh well, I suppose bad luck always strikes when you least need it… Oh that didn't sound right, did it. No one needs bad luck, ever."

The food runner arrived with Zelda's meal, and Martha stood. "I'll let you eat," she said.

"Wait," Zelda said. "Were there other Christmas 'incidents'?"

"Not that I was aware of… you might talk to Rhonda. Your grands consulted her… I think."

"Rhonda?"

"Oh, yes, Rhonda Phillips. She lives on the other side of the village. I don't know if she's still all there, if you know what I mean. So, take everything she says with more than one grain of salt."

56

Zelda watched Martha walk away, feeling as if the woman's words had left her with more questions than answers.

She hadn't known of the Christmas problems, and that didn't particularly bother her. The grands were always close-lipped when it came to bad news.

But had the 'incidents' caused the ending of the annual party? If people were getting sick from the food... Zelda didn't answer that question. She was simply happy that she had hired a caterer.

Zelda drank a second pint, because the first one had deadened the pain in her arm. Then she drove back to the manor in the near dark. She expected to see the reindeer and other lawn ornaments scattered about, but to her surprise and joy, nothing was out of place. They were all lit too.

She entered the manor with a smile. Her arm and shoulder hardly ached. If she could manage a good night's sleep, she would be thoroughly pleased with herself.

She stopped in the library to pour herself a dram of whiskey. Luckily, several bottles still inhabited the cabinet. Then, she happened along to the kitchen. Everything was in its place. With her dram, Zelda took a pain pill. While she was pretty sure she wasn't supposed to take the pill with alcohol, she threw it back anyway.

She didn't believe she'd had enough to make a difference, and at worst it would make her sleep well.

Turning off the light, she went to bed. Sleep arrived quickly. She didn't dream.

Morning light stole through the bedroom.

Her arm throbbing, her shoulder stiff and sore, Zelda rolled to the side and pushed herself to a sitting position before she... screamed.

Chapter Seven

The characters perched at the end of her bed weren't real. They were merely heads, but finding Santa and the Snowman staring back at her unnerved Zelda.

What in the world were those heads doing in the bedroom, and how in heaven's name, had they arrived? She had heard nothing during the night, but that might not be unexpected after the whiskey and medication. Yet, she had never been a terribly deep sleeper.

She should have heard someone delivering the heads. Even as her scream died, she found her anger growing... and along with the anger came a healthy dose of fear. If someone had stolen into her bedroom without her knowledge, well, that was a frightening thing, wasn't it? She jumped out of bed, not bothering to touch the heads. If she was going to call the police, she wanted them to see the evidence of a break-in.

The heads meant that someone had been in her house, in her bedroom, and that certain knowledge almost turned Zelda into a quivering blob. The heads were meant to scare her, and they had performed their roles ably.

And if the person involved was still around? She looked around the bedroom for a weapon. Since the bedroom had a fireplace, she decided on the poker. She wasn't sure she was strong enough or angry enough to hit someone — but she was scared enough. She grabbed her phone and dialled even as she left the room.

Zelda was on the phone to the police as she descended to the first floor. It was at the bottom of the stairs that she found several reindeer looking up at her. She was about to pass them, when she stopped and stared. The reindeer's cheerful smiles had been modified with some sort of paint and instead of harmless helpers, they took on an evil leer. They were decidedly not the helpful servants of St Nicholas. They looked positively fiendish. She sped past them, as if they were somehow going to attack.

In the kitchen, Zelda looked at the pain pills and decided against taking one. Put on hold after explaining that she was not under attack, she started water for tea and put her phone on "speaker" so she could use both hands. The throbbing arm looked all right to her.

At least outwardly it did, although she couldn't see through the bandage and didn't fancy taking it off.

She glanced at the basement door and was glad to find it closed, which caused her to check the back door. It was locked… and the front door… also locked. That didn't make sense unless the person who had delivered the heads had a key to the manor. Realizing that caused Zelda to shiver. If someone else had a key, then she wasn't safe. Returning to the kitchen, she cursed the police. Couldn't they answer her call?

As she entered the kitchen, she found the tea kettle screaming. As steam poured out, she hurried to the stove. Flames licked up the sides of the kettle. How had that happened? She had not turned the burner to 'high'. At least, she didn't remember doing that. And, it wasn't her habit to do that. She turned off the burner and moved the kettle, careful not to burn herself in the process.

She would have to let the kettle cool a bit, and she told herself that she was lucky the kettle hadn't burned through or melted or something. Would that cause a fire? She wasn't sure. Where were the bobbies? She was about to ring off when a woman's voice came over the phone. Thank god, someone had decided to answer.

For ten minutes, Zelda explained what had happened and why she needed a detective to come to the manor. She wasn't expecting Sherlock Holmes. She simply wanted someone to help. At the end of the ten minutes, the person on the other end suggested that Zelda take photos of the damage and send them to the police who would review them. Zelda found that solution less than satisfactory, but she knew it was the best she was going to get. Thanking the woman, Zelda went about making tea. If she was going to submit pictures, then there was no hurry.

Sipping tea, Zelda rubbed her sore shoulder. That reminded her that she had meant to search through the basement when she cut her arm and had to leave the manor. Should she continue her examination of the basement? She frowned. She didn't want to go into the basement. Something down there didn't feel right.

Her time could be better spent getting the locks changed, right? That thought made her smile. No need to check the basement yet.

She grabbed her phone and searched for a locksmith. Certainly, they weren't as busy as the police. Three calls later, a man named Mac promised to be there within two hours. That suited Zelda. But it also caused her to act. She had to take photos before the locksmith arrived.

Zelda had forgotten all about the figures on the lawn. What did they look like? She grabbed her tea and left the kitchen.

The pictures in the house were taken quickly. As soon as she had completed that task, she changed into jeans and a sweatshirt and carried Santa and the Snowman heads down the stairs. She opened the front door, half expecting to cringe at what the vandals had done to the outside. To her surprise, the lawn decorations were fine — with the exception of the heads and the reindeer. She replaced the heads the best she could. It seemed that every time the heads were removed, another dent or problem was added. Putting them back on kept getting harder. She tried to somehow hide the altered reindeer among the unaltered ones. Mixed in with the others, the evil reindeer didn't seem so threatening.

Satisfied, she returned to the manor and carefully locked the door, half wondering why she bothered because if there was a person with a key, they wouldn't be kept out. She hoped that person only worked at night, by which time the locks would be changed.

Zelda finished another cup of tea and avoided the basement until the locksmith arrived.

Mac was a fat man with an unsuccessful beard. He simply didn't have the wherewithal for a good beard, sporting big gaps in his white whiskers.

But he was jolly enough, and he liked the decorations, both inside and out. He didn't ask why Zelda needed new locks, which suited her to a tee. And while his eyebrows rose when she asked him to change the one on the kitchen door, he accepted her response of 'silver'. She guessed that he had heard that before. And he worked quickly, swapping them out in no time.

"There won't be no one gettin' through these locks," Mac said. "You'll sleep like a newborn."

The changed keys did make Zelda feel better. Whoever had the key to the previous locks would learn a hard lesson in the future. She was going to be safe. She was going to sleep. As she locked the front door after Mac left, she decided she would take a pill to ease her throbbing arm and sore shoulder. As she downed a pill, she noticed the basement door. It mocked her in silence. She knew she hadn't yet inspected the basement as she should, but was this the time for it? She took a step toward the basement and stopped.

Some small, niggling voice in her brain told her that she should leave the basement alone for the moment. Later, she could explore later. She needed sleep. She needed to heal. That was the advice her brain sent her. And she heeded the advice.

With the new locks, even if there were someone in the basement, she would be safe. All she had to do was lock the kitchen door. Yes, yes, that would make things right. Grabbing her new keys, she left the kitchen and carefully secured the door behind her.

After checking the front door, she marched up the stairs. Already, she was feeling a bit fatigued. Sleep couldn't be far behind. As she settled on her bed, she smiled. She was safe.

When Zelda woke, the room was dark except for the Christmas tree with its good-luck angel. She glanced at the clock and was amazed to find that it was midnight. She had slept away the entire evening.

For a moment, she considered getting up, but she frankly didn't feel like it. She wasn't hungry, and while her arm hurt, it didn't throb like before. She knew she should check out things, but the voice in her head said she was fine. She had new locks didn't she? But were they enough?

If the crazies had another way into the manor, and there was a good chance they did, then the new locks were nothing more than eyewash. She needed to do more. And that meant staying awake to catch the losers. She slipped out of bed, grabbed the poker, and shuffled in the dark to the first floor.

With the front door and kitchen door secured, she needed to find a place where she could see both doors. She pulled a chair from the great hall to a spot that offered lines of sight. Satisfied, she sat and clicked on her phone. She needed something to help her stay awake.

The trouble with using her phone was that the time was always on the screen. Zelda could see how slowly time passed. At the end of an hour, she determined that she needed some kind of early warning system. She pulled two chairs to lay in front of the doors. If someone came through, they would bang into them and fall or at the least make a racket. Brilliant. At the end of the second hour, she decided on a cup of tea.

She moved the chair, unlocked the kitchen door, and turned on the lights, which wasn't exactly stealthy.

The crazies would notice and not break in. Hour three found her in the loo, as might be expected. Hour four had her fetch her phone charger because the battery was fading. Hour five found her yawning. Her eyes closed. Hour six passed without notice.

The morning light filtered through Zelda's eyelids. She groaned as she moved her cramped body. Why had she decided to sit up all night? She looked around for reindeer or Santa heads. Nope, nothing, she wanted to cheer.

She started to move the chairs but decided against it. She would change first.

By the time Zelda reached the bedroom, she was feeling slightly less achy. As she entered, she smiled at the Christmas tree.

Then she stopped.

Where was the angel?

She was certain that the angel had been atop the tree when she went to sleep. But it wasn't there now. Where was it? Where was the little angel? A deep, deep cold invaded her. Where was the angel? She bit her lip and slowly turned all about, searching for it. Where could it have gone? Her hands shook, and her arm suddenly throbbed with the pain that she thought had ebbed. Her shoulder ached. Her brain felt like a hamster on an exercise wheel. It was moving as fast as it could go, and it was getting nowhere.

She needed tea. She needed food. She needed to find the angel. She needed many things. What she didn't need was the call that caused her phone to play its special ring tone. She didn't need that call at all.

Chapter Eight

The doctor didn't go into specifics. She merely stated that Zelda's mother had had an accident.

Nothing life threatening, just a fall off a chair that had resulted in a broken ankle.

Naturally, Zelda was the relative who had to step in and take the older woman home. The surgery nurse would deliver her to Zelda, and Zelda could take it from there.

Zelda's mother arrived in a wheelchair. With the help of the nurse, Zelda placed her mother in her car. Sliding behind the wheel, Zelda winced at the pain in her shoulder.

"I know what you're thinking," Zelda's mother said. "You're thinking that you don't have the time to babysit your mother, and you're right. All you have to do is drop me at my house. I'll be fine."

"Your ankle is broken, and you can't walk," Zelda said. "Precisely how do you expect to be able to do whatever it is that you expect to do... like eat."

"I have a prescription for a boot and a wheelchair. Drop me off, get me the boot and wheelchair, and all will be well. I am not helpless, Zelda. I'm merely inconvenienced at the moment. You have a party to prepare for. You do not need your mother taking up your time."

"Everything is already set up and running," Zelda lied. "The Christmas Eve party is still two days away. There is nothing to be done, I can babysit the manor or babysit you. Right now, I'll babysit you. I'll stay until I can have a nurse take my place."

Zelda's mother shook her head.

"I will not be responsible should anything happen to your little party. So, once you've set me up in my own home, then off you go."

Zelda recognized that her mother had gone from 'drop me off' to 'set me up', and that was telling. Her mother was indeed expecting more than a ride from Zelda, and that was fine with her. It would take a day or two to get her mother 'set up'. Otherwise, Zelda would never be forgiven. And Zelda did not want to face the backbiting should she not meet her mother's expectations.

"I'll get you into your house first," Zelda said. "We'll get into bed and start your pain medication. You heard the nurse. It's important to get ahead of the pain. What they gave you in the hospital will wear off soon."

"I feel so stupid. I got up on the chair to reach the top cupboard. You know how high it is. I reached, fell off balance, and tried to catch myself... It was like some sort of comedy gag."

Zelda gripped the steering wheel tightly.

"You got up on a chair?"

"Utterly clumsy. I suppose I should be thankful that I didn't snap my neck."

Zelda was happy that long sleeves hid the bandage on her arm. If she'd had to explain that, well, her mother would make something of the fact that they had both fallen. Coincidence? Her mother wouldn't think so. and she would start in on Zelda again... about the bad luck. Zelda might be half inclined to agree, but she wasn't going to let that thought open a conversation.

Getting her mother out of the car and into the house took all of the energy that Zelda could muster. Anyone watching would think them two of the dumbest people in the universe.

While her mother moaned and groaned, Zelda panted and gasped. Why she hadn't stopped for the wheelchair on the way mocked her every time her shoulder screamed in pain.

Yet, she struggled through. She placed her mother in bed and fed her a pain pill and half a glass of wine. With that, Zelda kissed her mother's cheek and left to retrieve the other items.

It wasn't until Zelda had found the items she needed and provided dinner that other thoughts slipped back in. As Zelda sipped a glass of cabernet in her mother's kitchen, she remembered the angel. What had happened to the angel from the Christmas tree? Zelda was damn certain the angel had not suddenly spread its wings and flown away. Where was it? And how did it get to wherever it had ended up? If she was the only person in the manor... She didn't finish the thought. She had to be the only person in the manor. She had changed the locks! No one could be there.

Except perhaps in the basement?

Because someone had grabbed her ankle? Well, it felt that way. And she had been distracted from going into the basement. So, if the basement were— She didn't finish the thought. It was either one or the other. And it was likely to be — well a person, the most likely explanation.

And if that was the case, then she just had to find that person. That nut-crazed person was just trying to get rid of her, that was all. But it was ZELDA who would get rid of THEM! Zelda felt cheered and momentarily animated by the notion. But there was no doing that from her mum's kitchen. But at least she could think about how she would do it.

The problem was, Zelda came back to the letter from the grands. The letter had warned her. The letter had mentioned some particular event in the past that had sullied Christmas on an annual basis. *But that couldn't be the real reason, could it?* That would mean there was some sort of energy, black energy that hated the manor, more than that, it hated *Christmas* at the manor, and that was impossible. Zelda couldn't believe in that. That was the stuff of ghost stories.

Ghost stories. Zelda couldn't bring herself to take ghosts seriously. Because if she did, she would be facing something that she had no way to banish. At least, she didn't think she had a way. Did she have one? In the guest bed, Zelda rued the fact that she had left her pain pills in the manor. Her arm still burned at times, and her shoulder complained every time she turned over. Yet, she managed to sleep in fits and starts, which prepared her for the morning when her mother demanded tea and biscuits and the newspaper.

Zelda did her best, and she managed to last till noon when the home nurse she had hired arrived. Zelda's mother complained about the switch of caregivers, but Zelda didn't let that sway her. She drove to the manor as fast as she could, fully expecting to find the Santa close behind a reindeer or perhaps the Snowman face down on the lawn. She was pleased to find the outside decorations in perfect order. Had the bobbies made passes during the night, scaring off the interloper? She didn't know, and she didn't care. All was well.

She had two notions as she unlocked the door. She had an angel to find. And she had a basement to scour. When she had accomplished those tasks, she would consider some pain killer. But not before. Her mind had to be clear.

Every light in the manor came on when she passed through the door. Zelda stopped... because that was not only wrong but impossible.

She stood in the entry, and her body began to shake. This could not be happening. The lights were on timers, and this was too early. What. Was. Going. On.

The alarm BLARED through the house.

Zelda fought the urge to run. She fought the fear exploding inside her brain. When something couldn't happen, it couldn't happen, could it? Was she in some kind of dream? Was she high on drugs. The alarm pounded on her. This was not something that could happen. She had a day and a half, and what if this happened during the party... She pulled out her phone and ran outside. There, she called Tod, the electrician. He didn't answer, so she left a message that included the blaring alarm. With that, she returned to the house.

And the lights were out.

Zelda wanted to cry. Her knees buckled, and she almost fell. It couldn't be happening. She balled her hands into fists and hammered her thighs. This had to stop. She had too much invested. Even as she pummelled herself, the alarm faded.

"No, no, no, no, no. no, no," she whispered.

She stepped backwards until her back hit the door. She wiped away the tears in her eyes. Then, she straightened her shoulders and told herself that there was no magic involved, nothing supernatural. Tod would fix the problem.

In the meantime, she had an angel to find. She pushed off from the door, her lips quivering. Despite her little pep talk, she was more afraid than she had ever been in her life. She started for the second floor, and up into her bedroom because that was the last place she had seen it. She didn't reach the bedroom. She stopped in the upstairs hall. She stopped and gaped and panted. She had found what she was seeking.

The angel dangled from a light fixture.

Its head had been bent to the side, as if its neck had been broken.

And it dangled from a hangman's noose.

Chapter Nine

Zelda stared at the angel for far too long. It was as if her brain had stopped working, stopped processing. Or maybe, she thought that, if she stared hard enough, the angel would disappear. She was seeing things, right? Hearing things? She blinked several times, thinking that the angel was a 'floater' one of those things inside the eye that distorted vision. If she blinked and tilted... No, the angel did not disappear.

Not knowing what else to do, she retrieved a chair from her bedroom and took it down. Its neck had been bent out of shape, and when she touched it, she felt a sort of shock, something that made her wipe her fingers on her sweatshirt. The little thing felt unclean. Not bothering to return the chair, she carried the angel to the kitchen door, and after unlocking it, put the angel in the rubbish bin. That was when she heard the laugh, the cackle, the evil sound of someone who enjoyed inflicting pain. She whirled and looked about. She was alone. She stared at the door to the basement. She needed to go there. She needed to assure herself that she was indeed alone. She had taken one step toward the door when the doorbell rang.

Tod apologized profusely as he passed Zelda. When she explained what had happened, he promised to find the cause and correct it. Which alarm had it been? She was certain it was the one in the kitchen. He said he would replace it. It would never bother her again. She gave him free rein of the house and retired to the library.

There she poured herself a finger of whiskey. She considered a pain pill, but that seemed like overkill. She needed to stay awake. She needed answers.

Nursing her drink, Zelda walked outside and noted that the decorations were still upright and together, but the wind had changed. It was stronger and colder, and she supposed a change was coming. That was all she needed, bad weather. Hadn't enough gone wrong already? if the weather interfered with the filming....

By the time the whiskey was finished, Zelda's head had cleared. She had reached an impasse.

Either there was someone clever enough to go in and out of the house at will and do all manner of scary things, or the house was somehow haunted by an evil energy. She remembered the grands' letter. What had happened so many years ago? And why did it matter now, at Christmas? More, what could she do about either possibility. If it was a clever, despicable human, well, she would catch him sooner or later. If it was an evil spirt? She had no real answer for that.

Or did she?

What had Martha said? Rhonda Pillbury? Wasn't that the name Martha had given her?

And what power might Rhonda have? What might she know that could be useful for Zelda? That was a mystery within a mystery. And the only way Zelda might find out was to find Rhonda. On the other side of the village? Was that right? Zelda berated herself for not listening as she should have. The wind bit her, and she retreated into the manor. At least, the heat was working.

She returned to the library and poured herself another bit of whiskey. Hadn't people since time immemorial called whiskey "liquid courage"? She needed courage, liquid or otherwise.

Zelda had returned to the kitchen by the time Tod had finished. He told her he had checked every relay and every breaker, and they all tested clean. He had replaced the offending alarm and run all the timers. Everything was exactly what it should have been. He reset the timers anyway, just to be sure. As far as he could see, the manor was in great shape — electrically. Zelda thanked him and walked him to the door. It was there that she asked if he knew Rhonda Pillbury.

Tod shook his head.

"But there is a Rhonda Phillips in town," he said. "An odd duck by all accounts. When I was young, we used to call her a witch. You never wanted to be caught in her back yard at night. Whenever a cat went missing, we said that Rhonda had used it as a sacrifice to the evil Satan she worshipped."

"She worshipped Satan?" Zelda asked.

"I don't think so. But the rumour was enough to keep us out of her yard, even when the apples were ripe." Tod laughed. "It's amazing what a good rumour can do."

After Tod left, Zelda looked up Rhonda's address. Armed with that and the GPS system in her car, Zelda set off, carefully locking all the doors before she left. Perhaps the locks would help. Thick grey clouds rolled toward her as she drove.

She was no expert, but it looked like snow, lots of snow. Or rain. She would settle for the rain if she could get it.

Rhonda Phillips looked like a witch — at least to Zelda. The old woman was skinny in the extreme, with a crooked nose and long, stringy, grey hair. She was bent over, as if she had smoked cigarettes for a century, and she wore a black dress straight out of some Brothers Grimm fairy tale. She didn't smile when she saw Zelda. Rhonda merely turned and walked away, leaving the door open. Zelda entered and closed the door and wondered if she was doing the right thing.

"You'll find water and tea in the kitchen," Rhonda called to Zelda. "Fetch me a cup."

Under other circumstances, Zelda would have told the old woman to 'fetch' her own tea. But in these circumstances, Zelda felt it better to acquiesce. There was an old saying about flies and vinegar and honey. Zelda would try to be honey.

The kitchen was old and dirty; filled with potted plants, mostly dead, that littered the window sill over a sink that needed to be replaced. Zelda felt the same sense of slime she had felt with the Angel, and that bothered her. What was it about the filth that was so off-putting? She couldn't be sure. She made two cups and carried them to the tiny parlour, what had to be a parlour, off the main hall. Rhonda sat in a rocker, a blanket over her knees. The gloom did nothing to hide her ugliness, which seemed a shame to Zelda.

"There's wood by the back door," Rhonda said. "Make me a fire."

Rhonda's tone made Zelda feel like a servant, which she was decidedly not. Yet, she fetched two small slabs of wood, added kindling she had found next to the fireplace, and finally struck a match that lit the small pile. It was a tiny fireplace for a tiny room, and when Zelda was finished, Rhonda simply handed over her cup without a word. Zelda understood the gesture. More tea. When Zelda delivered the second cup, she noticed that Rhonda had moved her rocker closer to the fire. Well, the old crone wasn't an invalid. And she might have thanked Zelda, might have. Rhonda didn't.

"You're one of them, aren't you?" Rhonda asked

"One of whom?" Zelda answered.

"A Livingston. You live in the manor."

"I don't actually live there."

"I should say not, not during Yuletide."

"What do you mean by that?"

"I mean, you're not the first Livingston who's come to ask about the curse."

Surprise spread Zelda's face. Who else had come to the old crone.

"Not your parents," Rhonda continued. "Your grands. They were the ones who started the curse, so naturally they came."

"I don't believe you," Zelda said. "They would never come here."

"You came, didn't you?" The crone smiled. "Some bad things happening out there? Some evil things? Some scary things? Some things that couldn't possibly happen?"

"What do you know," Zelda demanded. "Tell me!"

"You're haunted, lass. You're haunted by someone who likes to scare people, who likes to harm people. Figgy pudding."

The crone drew out the last two words, as if they needed emphasis.

"I'm not scared," Zelda lied.

"Oh, you're scared right enough. And you came because you don't know how to rid yourself of the ghost."

"I don't believe in ghosts."

The crone chortled. "No, but they believe in you!"

Zelda felt her embarrassment rise up her neck and into her cheeks. What was she doing? She was bantering with some ancient, nasty woman about ghosts? That was bonkers, bloody insane. She put down her cup.

"And now you're angry," Rhonda continued. "That's not a bad thing. Before you leave, I'll tell you how to be rid of him."

"Him?"

"Aye, your grands were insistent upon that. I'll tell you what I told them. There's something that ties the ghost to the house, something physical. It's like an anchor. It keeps him there. You find the anchor, and you move it, and the ghost goes with it."

"There is no anchor. Believe me, I've been through the house a dozen times, and there's nothing like that."

"I'm sure your grands thought the same thing. Which means that it's not lying around like a rug. It's hidden somewhere, and it won't be easy to find. But when you find it, you'll know it."

Zelda stood.

"I came here hoping to get some practical advice. Instead, I get this rot about anchors and ghosts and evil. I should have known better."

"Oh, you know better, or you will. Or you can be like your grands and shut down the manor for the Yuletide."

"There are only two more days till Christmas. I'm sure I can survive."

The crone cackled.

"And sometimes, they keep you alive longer, just to inflict more pain."

Zelda didn't bother answering. She turned and left without another word. As she drove to the manor, she chastised herself for being such a gullible person. She was acting like one of the characters in a Beeb show.

Despite all logic, she had gone to a clearly deranged woman for help. That was A-one idiocy. She had learned nothing. She was no nearer finding the source of the manor's ills than she had been before. She parked her car and started for the front door even as the first cold snowflakes struck her cheeks. Snow. As if she didn't have enough troubles.

Inside, Zelda remembered that she didn't have any food in the manor. She was tempted to hop into her car and drive into town, but that didn't appeal much, not in the snow.

Instead, she poured herself another whiskey and unlocked the kitchen door. Behind her the Christmas lights sprang to life, but unlike earlier, this was the proper time for the lights. They were supposed to be on.

That made her feel a bit better.

She had taken one step into the kitchen when the alarm BLARED on. The sudden sound made her jump and then spin to the noise. Anger surged through her. Tod had replaced the alarm not once, but twice. How incompetent was he? Zelda grabbed a chair and shoved it under the alarm. As she had done before, she opened the alarm in order to remove the battery. But there was no battery. She was stumped. There had to be a battery, right? The noise was deafening, and she didn't have time to debate the issue. She undid the catch and pulled the alarm off the wall. It came easily since...

It no longer had any wires leading to it.

She held the disconnected alarm for five seconds before it shut off as quickly as it had come on.

Zelda stared hard at the alarm, but it didn't give up the secret of how it could make noise without power of any sort. It was perfectly against the laws of nature. And yet, she was pretty sure she had not imagined the episode. She stepped off the chair and carefully set the alarm on the table. She now understood why Tod had been so sure the alarm wouldn't go off again. It couldn't if it wasn't wired with electricity. She wanted to get on the phone and yell at Tod, but she believed that wouldn't do any good.

How could it if her problem was beyond 'nature'? She picked up her glass and swirled the whiskey.

Her arm suddenly throbbed. Her shoulder ached.

She looked at the basement door.

And shook her head.

Not this night. Now, that the alarm was silenced, she could hear the wind whipping around the manor. To Zelda, it sounded like a major storm. She didn't want to hear it or listen to it. The only snow she needed was the snowman on the lawn.

What she really needed was sleep. After the angel and the crone and the alarm, she felt worn out. She shook out the last pill hospital had given her, but she didn't take it right away. First, she made sure that the kitchen door to the outside was locked. Satisfied with that, she dragged a chair to the basement door and laid the chair on its side. It wouldn't keep the door closed, but it might slow up someone.

Then, she took her pill and locked the kitchen door that led to the rest of the house. She stopped in the library to freshen her drink. Then, armed with the whiskey, she went to her bedroom. It too was lockable, and she locked it with the keyring she had managed to remember.

Ready for bed, Zelda sat against the headboard and listened to the wind.

She looked at the Christmas tree and immediately missed the angel. The image of the mangled angel made her wipe her hand on the comforter. There was one more day until the party, and she was not at all sure that it would be a success. Sipping the whiskey, she decided that perhaps, just maybe, it might be a good idea to chase down the supposed 'anchor', the thing that kept the supposed 'ghost' from leaving. Her eyes closed.

The pill was taking effect. She shook herself and opened her eyes.

The man leered at her from the foot of the bed.

Chapter Ten

Zelda stared for a second before she blinked, and after the blink, the man had disappeared.

What?

He had been there an instant before. Scruffy beard, lank hair, black clothes, chilling leer, she had seen it all. But now, he was gone! Frustration raced through her. she balled her hands into fists as tears came to her eyes. She fought the sobs rising in her throat, but they came anyway.

Zelda could not control the chills racing through her body. She shivered from toes to hair follicles, or so it seemed. There was a cold glob in the pit of her stomach, and tears forming in her eyes. A sudden pain seared her arm. Her ears rang with some unidentified tone. A foul odour washed over her, an odour that made her wrinkle her nose in disgust.

It reminded her of a grave, of something mouldering and decaying. It singed her nose. Disgusting.

Breathing through her mouth, Zelda gulped whiskey. Perhaps burning whiskey would wash away the ghastly smell.

Then, even as the whiskey caused more tearing, the odour disappeared. Disappeared? How? She wondered if she was losing her mind? Was the whiskey affecting her brain? She stared straight ahead, half expecting the leering man to pop up and laugh like a hyena. Her brain felt slow, addled. What was happening? She needed sleep, and she was certain sleep was coming.

She finished the whiskey and turned off the light by the bed. Scooting under the covers, she blinked at the Christmas tree and heard the wind, the cold wind that made her sink deeper under the covers. She told herself she would solve all the problems in the morning. Morning would be soon enough. Sleep dropped upon her.

The dream was disturbing on many levels. In the dream, she was running, and she wasn't sure exactly where she was. But she knew why she was running. The scruffy man in black was chasing her, laughing in that horror-movie way, as scary as a witch at midnight. And he was catching up.

Zelda ran as hard as she could, panting, her lungs burning, but she wasn't getting away. The leering man grabbed her by the neck and drove her down into... sand. Where had the sand come from? She couldn't turn her head. The man held her head in the sand, and she couldn't breathe. She couldn't breathe at all. Her lungs were about to explode. She struggled. She pushed as hard as she could. And her mind was shutting down. Sand filled her lungs. Something was desperately wrong.

She woke to find the pillow over her face.

Chapter Eleven

Panic surged through Zelda. For a moment, she felt as if the pillow was being held against her face, suffocating her. Despite a push, the pillow didn't move. And she was suffocating, really suffocating. She couldn't breathe! She shoved the pillow, and it moved, falling away.

Zelda gasped, sucking in all the air her lungs could handle. She sat up, coughing, gasping, needing more oxygen than her lungs could process. Fear drove her breathing, and it seemed as if it took ten minutes to calm down. She looked around the room, scared that she would spot the leering man peeking out from behind the Christmas tree. In the dark, she could see next to nothing, but she could hear the wind. That hadn't dissipated. Her heart slowed from its breakneck beating. She shook and sweated and hugged herself.

She couldn't seem to shake the dream, the feeling of being face down in the sand, the pillow over her face. As she calmed, she lowered herself to the bed and stared at the ceiling. She had no idea what time it was, and she didn't want to look at the clock. She was afraid to move her gaze.

She stared and waited, and knew that sleep wouldn't come again this night.

Luckily, the dawn wasn't far away, and as light crept into the bedroom, Zelda slipped out of bed. Shadows hid everywhere, and they frightened her even if there was nothing in them. She dressed, frequently looking over her shoulder, praying that she wouldn't see the leering man. She listened for the alarm, but there was nothing but the wind. Sniffing, she was pleased that the foul odour of the night before was gone. She still missed the angel, lucky angel.

On the first floor, Zelda looked out the window, afraid that the lawn decorations had once again been vandalized. But she saw only the snow and the wind. There was far more snow than she'd thought possible. And the wind sang as it whipped flakes past Santa and the Snowman. She shivered at the sight, before she prayed that the Santa wouldn't fly away along with his reindeer.

Zelda unlocked the door to the kitchen and pushed it open, ready to hear the alarm or see Mr. Scruffy.

Pleased that nothing happened, she moved on to the tea kettle. After the dream, the suffocation, she needed tea, hot tea. She could use something to eat, but she hadn't bothered to stock the larder. Getting out in the snow didn't look wise either. Tea would have to do. As the water heated, she avoided looking at the door to the basement. She had come to understand that it was a bad place, a really bad place. It seemed that every time she sought to enter it, something happened. Why was that? She remembered the fall, the cut, the slam — all because she had tried to go down into the basement.

Basement.

But there was nothing there, right? An empty room and an empty coal bin. What else was there?

Something.

The tea soothed her nerves. Energy flowed into her muscles. She felt a need to do something because she sort of knew that if she didn't do something, the next day's party would be an utter failure. If it wasn't an alarm, it would an odour or blinking lights, or reindeer that looked like devils.

The crone had told her. The crone said the anchor was somewhere in the manor.

But to find it, Zelda had to believe the anchor existed. Didn't she? She sipped tea and looked at the basement door. Her eyes widened as the door bowed, stretching toward her, as if some huge hand was pushing, making the door stretch like a balloon.

She blinked, and the door shrank back to its normal configuration. Fear, brutal fear, danced along her spine. The meaning of the door seemed obvious. Something big, something monstrous was in the basement, and it wanted to get out. If she dared the basement, that thing, that power would overwhelm her. It would bury her face in the sand.

Zelda stared at the door.

Did she dare?

What happened if the party failed, if the filming failed?

She would lose everything.

Did she dare?

She didn't see any way around it.

Zelda stood. She needed to search for the anchor, but she couldn't just rush down the stairs. She was afraid that the leering man was in the basement, the thing she needed to overcome, the thing that had tried to suffocate her. And she wanted to be smart about it. She finished her tea and went on a scavenger hunt.

The heat died while Zelda changed clothes. She put on her oldest jeans, shoes, and sweatshirt. But she knew immediately that the furnace was no longer working. The fierce cold outside sapped the heat from the manor. She shivered in the sudden draughts, and she knew that the heat wouldn't come back until she had either won or lost to the leering man. In the library, she found a flashlight, and to her surprise, it worked. She looked for a moment for some sort of religious artefact. She thought perhaps having a cross on her person might help. But she couldn't find anything. What she did do was drag a chair to a Christmas tree and take off another angel. It was a lesser angel than the one that had been hung, but it would do.

She stuffed the angel into her waist and headed for the kitchen. The cold grew more intense. She thought about grabbing a knife, but she didn't really think a knife would work against leering ghost man. Besides, the last time she'd taken a knife into the basement, it hadn't turned out well. She faced the door and took a deep breath.

The stench flowed over her in waves, and she coughed as her eyes stung. She stepped back as if pushed. The smell was palpable. With a little cry, she pulled her jumper to her face and breathed through the fabric. For a moment, she thought perhaps the ploy wouldn't work. But it did.

She found that she could handle the scent if she filtered it. It was crazy, and she was glad there wasn't anyone around to see her.

She stepped forward, and the door bowed for a second time. The effect was especially disconcerting and she fell back. It was flat scary. What kind of thing could make wood act like rubber? The desire to flee raced through her head. So, did the knowledge that she needed to have a Christmas party, and she was running out of time. In less than eighteen hours, there would be either a party or a bankruptcy.

"NO!" Zelda called out loud pushing the rubbery door again "I'M COMING FOR YOU"

The door flattened, and as it did, the alarm on the table came alive. The BLARE echoed off the walls, hammering at her brain. And what was happening couldn't be happening because the alarm wasn't attached to any power supply.

But it was happening.

She knew that as long as she didn't move, the alarm would continue. An AHA moment ignited in her brain. That was the purpose of the alarm, to make her stop. Anything that made her stop moving into the basement would continue. She jerked open the door and turned on the lights, which came on. That helped. She looked down the steps. Her arm throbbed. Her shoulder didn't want to move.

The noise beat at her back. She slid the torch into her waist band and grabbed the handrail. Holding the jumper over her mouth and nose, hanging onto the railing, she moved one step at a time. She half expected a hand to grab her ankle and make her fall, and she was ready for it.

Right foot down, left foot down. She stared ahead. Leering ghost man was down there somewhere... right?

Halfway down, the alarm stopped, which was a blessing. Zelda felt her teeth stop hurting. She pushed ahead. At one point, she thought she felt someone brush her ankle. She stopped in her tracks, and the feeling disappeared. It took far longer than normal, but she made it to the floor without incident. She smiled. Success seemed assured. All she needed to do was find... an anchor. But... what the bloody hell was the anchor?

She looked around the large room and saw — nothing. There was a door and a doorless square chute. She could reason that the anchor had to be behind the door that led to the coal bin, and as far as she knew the coal bin was empty also. Well, she was pretty sure the bin was empty. Straightening her shoulders, she started for the coal bin.

The CACKLE seemed to come from everywhere, and it was the leering man's cackle. She stopped again to survey the room. She didn't see anyone, but that didn't mean anything. A ghost could appear... anywhere. Seconds later, satisfied that she was un-assailed, she started again. This time, the CACKLE didn't stop her.

She marched forward until she came to the door. When she reached for the doorknob, the odour struck again. But with her jumper over half her face, she was prepared. She wanted to laugh. If that was the best the leering man could do, well, she could manage. She pulled open the door and faced the utter blackness of the empty coal bin. Zelda pulled out her torch and flicked it on. The torch's light was feeble, but it helped some-what. As she stepped into the bin, the cold intensified.

It was as if she were standing out in the freezing snow. Her hand shook, and the light bobbled up and down along the far wall. While the bin was small, she wanted to make sure it was totally empty. She shone the light into the corners, looking for something that she couldn't describe. She supposed that she would know it when she found it. The anchor.

Two steps into the bin, the door SLAMMED shut behind her. Zelda's response was instant.

She spun and rushed to the door. Grabbing the knob, she twisted it for all she was worth, and while the knob worked, she couldn't push it open. The door was stuck somehow.

She tried pushing again with her good shoulder, but that didn't work. She pushed harder and found the door unyielding. Panting through her jumper, she stepped back. The torch's light was more feeble than ever, and the cold nipped at her nose. She knew, knew she had to get out of the bin quickly. Fear shot through her brain. What if she didn't get out? She would freeze to death in the bin. The partygoers would find her lifeless body and wonder what the bloody hell she was doing in the coal bin. It was insane.

Then, she reminded herself that she had come into the bin to look for the anchor. She should complete that task and then tackle the door — because once she got out, she wasn't coming back in. She moved around the bin, playing the light over every wall, every corner, even the ceiling. The coal chute had been boarded up, and the cover was secure. If the anchor were in the chute... She didn't complete that thought. The anchor had to be accessible. That made sense. Satisfied that she had succeeded in only getting her shoes covered with coal dust, she turned back to the door.

Her breath steamed in the cold as she grabbed the knob which seemed frozen. She twisted and pushed... nothing. She pounded the door and yelled.

"HELP! HELP!"

Then, she realized that she was all alone in the manor, and she had locked everything up, just in case someone *was* out in the snow storm waiting for their chance to get in.

Zelda stepped back and stared at the door. Like the cold, fear was seeping into her bones. As the torch faded, the darkness grew, and she knew that in darkness, she wasn't liable to get out. Then she did the only thing she could think to do, something she had seen on the sets where she had worked. She backed up as far as she could. Then, she sprinted at the door and kicked with both feet.

To her surprise, the jamb splintered, and the door sprung free. She landed on her side, which hurt, but she was excited. She had managed to open the door. Standing, she realized that she had covered herself in coal dust. But she discovered the odour had abated. She no longer needed the jumper over her face. She laughed. She was winning, wasn't she? She stepped out of the coal bin and discovered that she had injured an ankle. The pain was excruciating, and she almost fell.

CACKLE

She shivered, and it wasn't just because of the cold. She spun, expecting to find the leering man behind her. But the room was still empty.

It couldn't be empty.

The anchor had to be there somewhere.

CACKLE

She felt the urge to bend over and cry, to give up. Her arm throbbed. Her fingers ached with cold. Now, she had an injured ankle to go with her shoulder. She wasn't winning, she was losing. No, she couldn't lose, not now.

She looked around the room, past the pipes that indicated where the washer and dryer had been hooked up. The laundry had been done in the basement, if she remembered correctly. When had that changed? Past the pipes was the square chute. What had that been?

Then, she remembered, or thought she remembered. The manor had had a dumbwaiter. The door to it was still in the kitchen. In the old days the laundry had descended and risen by dumbwaiter. Simple and efficient.

But while she knew where the door to it was, upstairs, where was it here? She didn't see one. Hobbling, she started over toward it.

CACKLE

The lights flicked out, leaving Zelda in almost total darkness. The torch's dim light illuminated almost nothing. In the cold, in the mostly dark, Zelda dragged her bad foot and reached the dumbwaiter. She shone the light over it as the alarm BLARED into life in the kitchen. Then, she saw where there had once been a door. Someone had removed the door and fitted a piece of wood in its place. Zelda stared at the wood and wondered what to do. She was loathe to kick the wood, since that might injure her good ankle. Instead, she lowered herself to her knees and grabbed the torch. She gripped the torch tight and slammed the butt end of it into the panel.

CACKLE

The stench blew past her.

She hammered the panel a second time, and it cracked.

CACKLE, CACKLE, CACKLE. A third blow split the panel, and she managed to pull loose the pieces.

What she stared at was a black hole. She didn't want to reach into the darkness. She tried to shine the torch inside, but it was too big to see the bottom.

BLARE

CACKLE

Frigid, she was finding it difficult to think. She stretched her hand toward the hole and stopped. What was at the bottom of the dumbwaiter?

Then, she got an idea. She pulled the angel from her jeans and fitted her hand inside. She found she could manipulate the wings a bit, enough to grasp something perhaps. Before she put the angel into the darkness, she kissed it — for luck.

She felt around and found something. Smiling, she pulled it out. She shone the torch on it and...

SCREAMED.

The angel held a dry, old, rat carcass.

Zelda SCREAMED a second time as she hurled the carcass across the room.

Wait, her mind said, maybe the carcass was...

No, Zelda told herself. The carcass was not the anchor.

Panting, breathing through her mouth, Zelda steeled herself and sent the angel into the hole again. She felt around and found something.

She was almost too frightened to pull out the thing. But she did, and to her joy, the Angel held a small, leather pouch.

If anything, the alarm grew louder, the stench fouler, and cold more frigid. Zelda laid the pouch on the floor and opened it. It was old but not ancient, and it opened easily. Inside, the torchlight found a razor, a comb, nail clippers, tweezers, tiny scissors, and pound coins. The items appeared to be in perfect condition, and she knew, knew deep inside, that this was the anchor. This tied the ghost to the manor.

Grabbing the pouch, she staggered to her feet. As she did, the torch died. But it no longer mattered. She had only to take the pouch out of the manor. That was all. She limped to the steps.

Cackle. The laugh was small. The alarm faded to nothing. The stench disappeared.

Each step was agony for Zelda, but she bit her lip and pushed, and in a couple of minutes reached the kitchen. It was still deathly cold, and there were no lights.

Feeling her way carefully, one hand along the edge of the wall, it was enough, in the gloom, to guide her. Grasping tightly onto the bag, she crawled up to the second floor.

In her bedroom, she put on her coat and grabbed her purse. When she glanced in the mirror, she spotted the leering man behind her. He disappeared because she was no longer so scared of him. She shook the pouch at the mirror.

"You're leaving," she said. "LEAVING!"

Outside, the snowman was missing his head and hat, and they were nowhere to be found. Santa seemed to be doing all right, but the reindeer were blown over. Zelda no longer cared. She would fix it later. She climbed into her car and tossed the pouch onto the seat.

The cemetery was next to a church, which Zelda thought was just fine. She parked her car and climbed out into the blowing snow. The snow wasn't so thick as before. Every bone and muscle in her body ached as she struggled into the cemetery. She had no idea whose grave was whose, and she didn't care. She walked to the end of the cemetery where the markers were small and labelled with just a name. Charity graves perhaps. She picked one and looked at the name.

STANLEY PARKER. She knew it wasn't the right grave, but she didn't care. Perhaps the church would help the ghost find rest. She dropped the pouch on the grave.

"Stay here," Zelda told the pouch. "Stay the bloody hell away from me."

She turned and dragged her foot through the snow. She thought she heard a disgruntled whining. It could have been the wind, but whatever, she didn't care. If this was the anchor then the old man was GONE from the manor. That was all she cared about.

But it's Yuletide.... the wind seemed to whine. I'm out in the cold. I'll freeze to death. Zelda did not care. She was guessing that had happened long ago.

EPILOGUE

"The house looks fabulous," Jeremy said as he uncapped the marker. "What should I write?"

"Whatever you bloody well please," Zelda said.

Jeremy bent over the cast on Zelda's ankle and started to write.

"I overheard Natalia say the cast is genius. They'll be able to work it into the story line."

"It's not a prop," Zelda said. "Don't write a novel."

"Never question genius," he answered.

"I won't when I see one."

"Ha, ha."

"Get me another wine."

"Yes, your highness. And I have to compliment you on the party. It's fab."

Zelda looked around at the guests, with their plates of food and drinks.

The film crew had been subtle and thorough, getting what they wanted. The house was warm and filled with Christmas cheer.

It wasn't perfect; there was still a rat carcass in the basement, along with a ruined door and a hole in the dumbwaiter chute. But those were things that would be repaired in the fullness of time.

"May I sign your cast?" Natalia asked.

"Better hurry," Zelda answered. "I get a boot next week when they can treat me properly."

"I won't count chickens before they're hatched, but this looks perfect. You did a masterful job."

"Thanks. It looks easier than it was."

As Natalia moved away, Devon arrived with a glass of wine in hand.

"Surprise, my love."

"Devon!" Zelda said. "You're here!"

"I had to bribe the pilot to leave an hour early. And even then, I nearly didn't make it," he said pulling her in close. "I had the devil of a time getting a car on Christmas Eve, and when I did I nearly went off the road up by that old graveyard. The fence was flattened and a maverick headstone nearly took me out. I had to swerve off into the side to miss the bloody thing."

Zelda gulped. Boxing Day, she'd take Rhonda Phillips a plate of food and a gift. On the way she'd find that blasted purse and take it with her. Rhonda would know what to do.

But for now, Devon had made it and his smile was perhaps the best Christmas present Zelda could ask for. He bent down and kissed her, and she felt warm all over.

"Merry Christmas," Devon said.

"Merry Christmas," Zelda answered, vowing that this would be first of many more merry ones, held right here, in the manor. She'd even throw a New Year's Eve party.

Just as soon as she'd talked to Rhonda.

THE END

I hope that you enjoyed this book.

If you are willing to leave a short and honest review for me on Amazon, it will be very much appreciated, as reviews help to get my books noticed.

Over the page you will find a preview of one of my other books, *The Haunting of Blakely Manor.*

Here is your preview of

The Haunting of Blakely

Manor

Prologue

Blakely Manor
Derbyshire
England 1998

Lord Henry Blakey swallowed the blue pill, looked at himself in the mirror, and decided that he looked handsome with grey hair. It was far better than the two-toned look he had sported last year. No wonder the women had stopped looking at him. Now, now, he had the distinguished look he desired. Now, the women noticed him. Just a few days earlier, a barista had given him a double shot of cream in his tea. That was proof positive. And if that wasn't enough, there was Shelly.

Shelly was more than a barista. Well, if he admitted the truth, she was the maid, but she had shown more than a bit of enthusiasm the first time he had taken her to bed. And she looked better than the barista—to him. That alone justified the tip he had given Shelly after their encounter. It was a tip. He made that explicit. He was not getting sex for money.

That would be unthinkable. He pulled in his stomach and studied himself. He reminded himself of an Earl many years removed whose portrait hung in the gallery of all the Earls.

That Earl had the svelte figure that he needed. Of course, that Earl had been the one to use the priest hole.

Few people knew about the priest hole. It was a space alongside the fireplace, barely large enough for a modern woman yet big enough for a man from a bygone era. When the Earl was a boy, he sometimes hid in the priest hole. He would play tricks on his friends. He would run into the room and slide into the priest hole. When the others entered, they would find the room empty. He'd always told them that he knew how to disappear.

Of course, that was after the first time he was shown the hole. His father had shut him in, and the Earl had more than a moment of terror in the complete dark — because he didn't know how to get out.

His father had left him in there for a minute that seemed like an hour. When the Earl was shown the hidden release, his father opined that the little minute of terror guaranteed that the Earl wouldn't forget where the release was.

He hadn't.

"There you are."

The Earl turned and smiled. "I thought you had left already."

His wife didn't smile. He told himself that modern plastic surgery did that to women… and men. Some of his contemporaries had tried facelifts, and none of them were the better for it. A face was supposed to wrinkle.

"You have to be out by nine tomorrow morning," she said. "They're sealing the house for the winter."

"I remember," he answered.

"You remember nothing. Now, give me a kiss, and I'll be on my way."

He kissed her cheek and watched as she left the room. He often wondered just how he had come to marry her in the first place. He went to the window and watched as she drove off in her little car, the one she said she had to have.

Then, he went back to his dressing table and took a blue pill. Something in his brain said he had already taken a blue pill, but he ignored the voice.

"There you are."

He turned, and Shelly skipped over to give him a kiss on the cheek.

She wore nothing but panties and bra, and she looked as sexy as his wife's fast car. She dropped her black purse and pink dress on the bed.

"My, aren't you looking good," she said, sliding her hand down his thigh.

He felt a stirring, and that was a good thing. He supposed those blue pills were worth the exorbitant amount he paid for them.

"I bet you're in the mood for something special..."

"HENRY!"

His wife's voice echoed up the stairs.

The Earl had no idea what his wife wanted, but he knew that if he were found in this situation, his wife would divorce him in a trice. But he had a solution. He pulled Shelly to her feet and led her to the priest hole.

As he went, he grabbed the purse and dress. He popped open the door and pushed her inside, adding her things.

"Not a word," he hissed. "I'll be right back."

"Please, no. I'm claustrophobic."

"Not a word!"

He closed the door and spun just before his wife entered.

"There you are," she said as she looked around the room. "Did you remember to pay the credit card? I do not wish to be embarrassed again."

"Of course, I paid it," he answered. "You came back to ask that?"

"I would have called, but you don't answer the phone."

"Of course, I answer the phone."

"Hah! Has the maid left already?"

"She's disappeared. After all, we're closing the manor." He grabbed his wife's arm and led her out of the room. "Where are you going again?"

"You remember nothing."

He escorted her to the front door and dutifully watched her drive off. He stood there a full five minutes, until he was certain she wasn't coming back. At that point, he felt a fever in his cheeks, and his vision seemed better than usual.

Smiling, he ran up the stairs. His Shelly awaited.

At the top of the stairs, he felt the first twinge. He stopped as pain shot across his chest and up his arm. What was this? For a long moment, he couldn't quite think.

He knew something was wrong, dreadfully wrong, but he didn't know what. By the time it dawned on him, it was too late.

His heart quit with a jolt that stopped all circulation. His vision went dark, and he fell backwards, tumbling down the stairs. By the time he reached the bottom he was utterly dead.

Inside the priest hole, Shelly tried to move. Panic was only one short minute away.

Chapter One

Blakely Manor
Derbyshire
England 2018

Alison stood before the manor and wondered. The main house was old, very old, dating back to the sixteenth century. It had been added to over the years, and it now featured four bedrooms and baths, including a master suite. According to the listing agent, the house hadn't been lived in for twenty years, and that meant it would be selling cheap. The listing agent had hinted that the sellers were very motivated to sell since the local council would soon be raising taxes. Alison wasn't worried about the taxes. She knew that the council would look favourably at a successful bed-and-breakfast, anything to bring tourists and tourist money to the area.

But the manor didn't look inviting from the outside. The shrubbery and grass had grown wild and tangled. The slate roof looked sturdy enough, but she would need to be there in a rain to make sure.

The leaded windows were intact, but they needed washing. The grime of neglect clung to the glass. Yet, she could picture the manor as she wished it to be.

Sparkling glass, fresh paint for the stucco, trimmed bushes, and a blue ribbon on the door. Yes, it could certainly become The Headlands B-and-B. She was pretty sure she could make a go of it, if she could contain her costs. She walked around the house and noted that the formal garden had almost ceased to exist. It must have been something at one time.

And she knew it could be transformed into a haven for quiet contemplation. The fountain in the middle would babble again. She knew where she would place several tables for afternoon tea and evening drinks. With the setting sun providing a glow, her customers would sit, sip, and dream. There was nothing wrong with dreaming.

Alison had been dreaming of a place like this for the ten years she had spent designing commercials for TV. She had come to hate that work. Although it paid well enough, it was a soul-sucking job that drained away her energy and faith. It seemed everyone in TV was some kind of sleaze-ball.

She couldn't count how many times some "celebrity" had made a pass at her. Some had gone beyond that before they were slapped. No, she wasn't that kind of girl, and that business was not for her.

From the garden, the back of the house appeared sound. There was a balcony, and she guessed that marked the master suite. She would be able to charge extra for the suite, and she imagined she could offer breakfast for two on the balcony, or perhaps twilight champagne. That would be a nice touch.

She looked around at the green hills and forests. The countryside would provide ample hiking opportunities for the adventurous.

And the surrounding villages would teem with curio shops and pubs. The council had sent her a list of museums and historical sites, and she would have maps produced for her guests. Simple and elegant.

She continued her tour of the grounds. Everything was neglected and in need of care. But she couldn't see anything that would translate into a major rework. She didn't have the money for rework.

While she intended to borrow a goodly sum, that money was meant for other bills. She didn't want to spend it on repairs.

In her car, Alison jotted some notes on her tablet computer. She had a decent idea of the money she might make in a year. With that, she knew how much she could afford to offer for the house. It was a fairly low number, but if the owners were as desperate as Alison was told, then they would accept. Of course, if they knew that she hadn't worked for two months after quitting her job, they might sense her own desperation and make a counter offer. From her car, she looked at the old place and hoped it was within her reach. She needed something.

Chapter Two

The pub was boisterous, filled with football fans who were yelling at the multiple TV sets hanging wherever one looked. Alison found the booth where Paul sat with one pint half-finished and the other getting warm.

"You're late," Paul said as Alison slid into the booth. He tapped his phone and slid it off the table and into his pocket.

"I was at the manor house, looking around," Alison answered. "And thanks for starting without me."

"Please, you can't expect me to sit here and do nothing."

"You weren't doing nothing. You were on the phone."

"And drinking, don't forget drinking."

"Let's not argue. I spoke to the listing agent, and he gave me some tips. So, the visit was well worth it."

"They accepted your offer? That's terrific." He held up his glass, and she toasted with him. "When can we get started?"

"I haven't made the offer yet. I will tomorrow. Then, we'll see."

"I'm sure they'll take the money. No one wants a huge, old house just sitting around going to the dogs."

"Peers are strange sometimes. They don't always act in their best interests. It's a pride thing, I think."

Paul grinned and grabbed her hand. "I can't wait till we open up World's End."

"World's End? I thought we had settled on The Headlands."

"Well, I've been thinking, and World's End seems more edgy, more like it's some kind of garden of Eden or something."

"Or some kind of hell."

"So, you don't like my ideas, now?"

"Of course, I like your ideas. I just thought we had gone through all this already. But if the name is still in the air, then, it's still in the air. Please, let's not argue."

He shrugged. "It probably doesn't matter anyway. Either name will do. I wonder which one bubbles to the top of an Internet search. That's important, you know."

"How do you figure that out? It's not alphabetical, is it?"

"No, the search engines have some kind of algorithm for returning information to the screen. I'll look into it. By the way, I have Jeff writing reviews for us."

"Reviews? We aren't even open yet."

"It's the biz, sweetheart. You need a lot of five-star reviews that potential customers will read. They can't all be five-star, because no one will believe that, but most of them must be high. And Jeff is a first-rate writer. You know that."

"I know he writes that Dear Abby type stuff for women. I don't consider that good writing."

"He gets paid, Alison, he gets paid. That means something."

"Yes, it means that we will be booked full with women who have sordid and dramatic problems."

"As long as they pay, what do we care?"

She shrugged.

"You're right. I don't care how dramatic they are as long as their credit is good and they don't complain about the food."

"They'll never bitch about my food, never."

He waggled his empty glass in front of her.

"Another?"

She nodded, and he slipped away. Did he really have his friend, Jeff, writing five-star reviews? In a way, she liked the idea.

Read the rest:

FIND IT ON AMAZON HERE

http://a-fwd.to/6kx4iyT

Other Titles by Cat Knight

The British Hauntings Series

The Haunting of Elleric Lodge - http://a-fwd.to/6aa9u0N

The Haunting of Fairview House - http://a-fwd.to/6lKwbG1

The Haunting of Weaver House - http://a-fwd.to/7Do5KDi

The Haunting of Grayson House - http://a-fwd.to/3nu8fqk

The Haunting of Keira O'Connell - http://a-fwd.to/2qrTERv

The Haunting of Ferncoombe Manor –

http://a-fwd.to/32MzXfz

The Haunting of Highcliff Hall - http://a-fwd.to/2Fsd7F6

The Haunting of Harrow House - http://a-fwd.to/6F83zVM

The Haunting of Stone Street Cemetery –

http://a-fwd.to/1txL6vk

The Haunting of the Grey Lady –

https://www.amazon.com/dp/B07DLH7ZVS/

The Haunting of Blakely Manor –

https://www.amazon.com/dp/B07FS8D6TF/

The Haunting of Rochford House –

https://www.amazon.com/dp/B07CGNSH7X/

The Haunting of Knoll House –

https://www.amazon.com/dp/B077ZRN1YZ/

Ghosts and Haunted Houses: a British Hauntings Collection –

https://www.amazon.com/dp/B07CXRPS83/

The Ghost Sight Chronicles

The Haunting on the Ridgeway - http://a-fwd.to/67hRaLu

Cursed to Haunt - http://a-fwd.to/61SzXlz

The Revenge Haunting. COMING SOON

About the Author

Cat Knight has been fascinated by fantasy and the paranormal since she was a child. Where others saw animals in clouds, Cat saw giants and spirits. A mossy rock was home to faeries, and laying beneath the earth another dimension existed.

That was during the day.

By night there were evil spirits lurking in the closet and under her bed. They whirled around her in the witching hour, daring her to come out from under her blanket and face them. She breathed in a whisper and never poked her head out from under her covers nor got up in the dark no matter how scared she was, because for sure, she would die at the hands of ghosts or demons.

How she ever grew up without suffocating remains a mystery.

RECEIVE THE HAUNTING OF LILAC HOUSE FREE!

When you subscribe to Cat Knight's newsletter for new release announcements Subscribe at
http://eepurl.com/cKReuz

Like me on Facebook

https://www.facebook.com/catknightauthor/

Printed in Great Britain
by Amazon